DIVA LAS VEGAS

* * *

Caroline Dries

Steve Dries

ISBN: 978-0-615-58479-9

contact: csdries@gmail.com

Chapter 1

I was naked and sweaty and *not* in the mood to walk in on someone rummaging through my locker.

"Excuse me, can I help you?" I used my bitchiest voice.

The woman flinched and straightened up to face me. "Just checking to see if you still keep some hooch around here." She managed a weak smile.

"Rachel!" I was almost speechless. "It's been years!"

She shrugged. "About that hooch . . ."

"Sorry, they made us quit drinking in here. We'll have to go somewhere if you want a drink."

She nodded somberly. "Let's go, then. My treat."

I reluctantly threw on some clothes and guided Rachel out the club's back exit. It was always nice to see an old friend, but I was in the middle of a shift, and it wasn't just any shift. With the orthodontist convention in town, I was walking away from a big sweaty wad of twenties. But a woman like Rachel Hannity wouldn't pop in out of the blue if it weren't important.

"Let's duck in over there," I said, pointing across the street at Bally's. We weaved our way through the casino and up to the esplanade connecting Bally's with the Paris casino. We stopped in at Napoleon's, a stodgy piano lounge that was pretty empty at this time of night. Rachel headed up to the bar to order us some drinks while I found us a secluded table.

When I'd started dancing a decade earlier, Rachel had been the It Girl at Cougar's gentlemen's club, where I still worked. As the top draw, Rachel became a millionaire before she was twenty-five, but then she upped the ante by landing one of the richest bachelors in town after making a private appearance at his birthday party. I hadn't seen her since her husband's funeral.

Rachel returned with a martini for herself and a glass of white wine for me. I would have preferred something stronger, but I let it slide.

"So what's going on?" I asked, trying not to seem too impatient.

She sighed. "For starters, I'm broke."

"You don't *look* broke." She was sporting at least five carats on her necklace alone, and her princess-cut engagement ring looked like it was on loan from Harry Winston. Or the Smithsonian. And her golden hair and perfect magenta nails had obviously received the recent attention of professionals.

Rachel took a long gulp of her drink and cleared her throat. "It's embarrassing. After George was killed, I kind of developed a little gambling habit. He left me a couple million, and I figured, what was the harm? It kept me busy. I was bored all the time, and they treated me nice at the casino. But I had a string of bad luck, and before I knew it I wasn't gambling with my own cash. I was signing papers to borrow money, and then after awhile there weren't any more papers to sign. It was firm handshakes in back rooms, and promises made in whispers. I guess I got in pretty deep."

"How deep?"

"About eight. Eight million."

"Ouch," I muttered.

"They're going to get my jewelry, my house, my car, everything. I know that. I don't really care about that stuff, honestly. But that won't cover the debt. The only thing I have left to give is ... myself."

I remained quiet. Rachel was in her late-thirties but looked about twenty-five, and if she took care of herself she was still a stunner who sported the best curves money could buy. I had no trouble believing that there were dozens of unscrupulous moneylenders who would allow her—or *force* her—to "work" off her debt. That's probably why they lent her so much money in the first place.

"Anyway," she continued, "I heard you finally started that investigation business you were always talking about, so I thought—"

I wanted to roll my eyes, but I stopped myself. My "investigation business" consisted of my probationary private detective's license and a half-dozen clients who'd stumbled across my half-assed internet website. It wasn't even a hobby, much less a business.

"You thought—" I prodded.

She looked down at her manicured fingers. "I want to sue Cody Masterson."

I tried to keep a poker face, but I'm pretty sure I failed. Three years earlier, Cody Masterson had been tried and acquitted for the murder of Rachel's husband George.

"For the murder?" I asked.

She nodded. She kept her eyes on her nails, which glistened under the soft candlelight.

I thought about it for a minute before responding. I had majored in criminal justice at UNLV, and that probably made me the most knowledgeable person Rachel could trust. But murders and lawsuits were a little out of my league. Okay, they were *way* out of my league.

"You'd win millions if you could prove wrongful death," I said gamely, "but he beat the charge in his criminal case."

Rachel nodded. "My lawyer said we need something more to take to a jury, or this isn't going to work. That's where you come in." She finally looked up.

"Makes sense," I said. "But why haven't you already sued him? It's been three years."

"I didn't need to. I didn't want to re-live all that, and I didn't get into debt until recently. I've tried to move on, but I don't see another way. I'm not going to become a sex slave."

I asked the obvious question. "Why me?"

She hesitated. "Well, my lawyer recommended a few other people, but it seems nobody wants to touch this."

Ouch, I thought.

"Plus, I trust you," she said.

I ignored her attempt to sugarcoat it. It was clear I was the fourth-string choice. "What's the time frame?"

"I need the money yesterday. They left me a note at my house, and the guys who came to take my car were sizing me up pretty good, like they were all going to take turns with me. It gave me the chills."

Rachel held my gaze. She was putting on a brave face, but it was obvious she was at the end of her rope.

I wanted to make sure she had thought this through. "Can I ask an obvious question? Why not just declare bankruptcy? Or call the cops?"

She smiled half-heartedly. "These people are good. When I started losing bigger and bigger, they helped make the pain go away. A little coke, a little more heroin. It helped, actually. But then they got me doing it on tape. And not just using. I kind of helped on the distribution end, you know, selling to some of my high society friends. Now they say I'm looking at federal time. These people are going to be paid, one way or another."

I grimaced. "The reason extortion is illegal is because it actually works."

She downed a healthy gulp from her glass. "Look, I know how this all sounds. I don't blame you if you're not interested. But at least talk to this guy first." She fished in her Chanel purse and handed me the business card of someone named Jeffrey Katz, Esq., a partner at Gilread Schwartz & Tannenbaum.

I did a double-take. "Jeff Katz?" I asked. "Forty-fiveish, looks kind of like a fat Billy Crystal?"

Her eyebrows rose. "Friend of yours?"

"Let's just say he's a friend of the family," I said, grinning.

Rachel chuckled knowingly. Her lawyer was a guy who loved naked ladies and gave good tips.

"Well, he's my lawyer, although I haven't paid him yet." She smiled sheepishly. "So, will you help a girl out?"

"Of course," I said, powerless to heed the alarm bells going off in my head. "I'll talk to your lawyer first thing tomorrow." I chugged my wine. If I'd been wearing a watch, I would have glanced at it.

"I hope you don't mind," I said, "but there's a convention in town and I really need the money."

Rachel perked up at this reminder of her past life and then shot me a quizzical look. "Let's see. July is normally slow—just Teamsters and real estate brokers, right?"

I smiled. "Actually, the orthodontists changed their party to July."

She squealed. "Why didn't you say so? Get out of here and get back on that stage!"

"I'll call you." I kissed Rachel on the head as I got up to leave. If there was something odd about ditching an old friend so I could dance naked in front of a room full of glorified dentists, it escaped me.

Chapter 2

I woke up late the next day in a strange mood. I made coffee and treated myself to a midday breakfast of bacon and peanut butter M&M's on my balcony overlooking the Strip. The orthodontists had been very kind to me, as expected, but in the light of day Rachel's troubles had me more than a little worried. Up until now the few jobs I'd taken had involved insurance cheats and men married to suspicious wives. I was pretty wet behind the ears, and even Rachel had admitted I wasn't exactly her first choice in private detectives. And Cody Masterson, the guy she wanted to sue, was part of a big time casino family. It made sense that no other detectives wanted to touch this case: detectives work *for* casinos, not against them. So why was I even thinking about it? Because Rachel had asked me to, and I was a sucker for a girl in trouble.

The first step was to talk to Jeff Katz, the lawyer. It was not a reunion I was looking forward to. I'd danced for him once or twice a week for three years before he decided to ask me out about a year ago. I hadn't been on a decent date in ages, so I foolishly said yes, in violation of club policy and common sense. After dessert I kissed him on the cheek and whispered in his ear that I wasn't going to sleep with him. He reacted like a wounded puppy, and since then I've felt awkward around him. I didn't feel bad about not sleeping with him, but I did feel a pang of guilt about ordering dessert. After that "date," our relationship gradually returned to its refreshingly simple ways: I would take his forty dollars, lead him into a back room, and then I'd take my clothes off and squirm around on his lap for a few minutes. I much preferred it that way, and I think he did too.

I put off calling the number on Jeff's business card for most of the day. By four o'clock, I had rationalized not calling him at all. It was Monday, and Jeff usually came into the club on Mondays. I'd probably see him at work. On my turf.

It was still about 90 degrees at eight that evening, so I gave myself some extra time to walk the six blocks from my apartment to Cougar's, which was a block off the Strip near the Bally's casino. I got myself together and headed out on stage to dance with Amanda, one of the few redheaded dancers who worked at Cougar's. It was early and still half-empty, so I had no trouble spotting Jeff sitting next to one of the catwalks off the main stage.

Like most men, Jeff wasn't particularly attractive, but he wasn't exactly ugly, either. He had the comfortably puffy body of a celebrity chef and facial hair that wasn't officially a beard but wasn't just unshaven stubble either. His black hair was thinning a little on top, and he tended to overdress for the occasion.

After our set I walked out to the floor to find Jeff. I was wearing a black thong and a tiny pink bikini top with Velcro fasteners, and Jeff smiled broadly at me when he spotted me walking in his direction.

"Hey, did you see who just left?" he asked.

I gave him my best smile. "No I didn't, honey."

"JaMarcus Collingsworth. He was an all pro last year for the Browns."

"Sorry I missed him," I said, truthfully. NFL guys tended to throw money around.

"He's a pass rusher. Very small for the defensive line, but he had like twelve sacks last year. He was on my fantasy team." He beamed proudly at his display of useless information.

"Hmm," I muttered. I realized I had actually danced for JaMarcus the night before, but I hadn't believed his story that he was a defensive lineman in the NFL. I just kept taking his twenties.

"JaMarcus *is* very small," I said. "Surprisingly so."

Jeff raised an eyebrow at my double entendre.

"In my job you learn intimate things about men that you don't necessarily want to know." No wonder JaMarcus had been trying to distract me with all those twenties last night. I could tell through his pants that the poor man was hung like a toy poodle.

"You danced for him?"

I nodded. "He was in here last night, too."

"At least he's got good taste in women," Jeff said approvingly.

I smiled coquettishly and began twirling my black hair with my index finger. That was my polite attempt to stifle all this small talk and get things rolling. I grasped Jeff's arms, hauled him up from his chair with both hands, and led him into the back room.

We had the room almost to ourselves. The back room was more dimly lit than the stage area and had a number of nooks and corners furnished with leather couches and overstuffed chairs. My friend Carlos, one of the bouncers, was leaning against the wall doing his best to look menacing. He nodded stiffly at me and his eyes flickered over my body momentarily before resuming their glazed-over stare. It was nice to have security back there, but sometimes Carlos could be a little rough with customers he thought were getting too friendly with me. Not exactly a great climate for tips.

I led Jeff to his usual chair in the far corner, where it was quiet enough to talk. The couches and bigger chairs were more comfortable for lounging, but Jeff knew better. Like a lot of regulars, he preferred a chair narrow enough to allow me to swing my legs around his middle to straddle him completely. I would get to that in a minute. I began the tease by pushing Jeff gently into the chair. I stood facing him and leaned over to rub his neck and shoulders while he inevitably gaped at my chest. As usual, he was smiling like a little boy on Christmas morning. While I rubbed his shoulders, I leaned slowly into his face so that my breasts pressed up against his cheeks. As I rubbed deeper I could feel his hot breath on my chest. I figured it was the perfect time to get some straight answers.

"Before we get too hot and heavy," I said softly, "can I ask you a couple of questions?"

He reluctantly came up for air. "Uh, of course." He would have said anything at that point. I eased his forehead back into my chest.

I continued rubbing his neck while I whispered in his ear, "How do you know Rachel Hannity?"

His head resurfaced again, his hair now slightly mussed. "What? I know her, yes. I do some estate work for her. Why?" He was babbling.

"She wants me to do a job for her. Something involving Cody Masterson."

Jeff jerked his head back and stared at me, thoroughly confused. "What are you talking about?"

"I have a little side business. I have a private investigator's license, and Rachel and I are friends." I hadn't told him about any of this during our so-called date.

Jeff let out a harrumph of befuddlement, but he seemed to be taking the news in stride. "Well, I'm sure you're great," he said. "But why do you need a side business? I've probably given you enough to retire on already."

I patted his head appreciatively. He was exaggerating, but it was true that I'd probably taken ten grand off him in tips in the last few years. "These things aren't going to look like this forever," I said, grabbing my silicone-filled D-cup breasts. "I need some way to make a living when they start sagging." According to Dr. Ruiz, that would never happen to my breasts, but the rest of my body wouldn't be so lucky.

Jeff seemed skeptical. "A private investigator, though? It seems a little mismatched for your, uh, talents."

I shrugged. It was none of his business what I did, but he was a good tipper so I decided to play along. "I didn't spend four years in college to get naked for a living. This job pays the bills, but I want to have a more normal life at some point. When I started college I thought I might want to become a cop, but the cops aren't going to hire someone with my work history. So I thought I'd go out on my own."

He nodded approvingly. "Makes sense. I didn't know you had a degree," he added.

"Yeah. I didn't plan it this way. I started doing this to help pay my tuition, and before I knew it I was pulling in five hundred a night. And that was ten years ago. Kind of hard to walk away from."

"Especially since you get to meet people like me."

"Um, yeah, that makes it all worthwhile." My sarcasm drew an injured look from Jeff. "Anyway, Rachel is in trouble. She says you're going to help her sue Cody, but you need someone to dig up some new dirt. Something the cops didn't have the first time around during the murder trial. Is that about the gist of it?"

"You hit the high points, yeah."

"So is there anything you haven't told Rachel about this?" I asked.

He frowned. "Like what?"

"Well, you and I both get paid by the hour. Sometimes we tell people only the things they want to hear. It's only natural."

Jeff's eyes had found my chest again, but he did his best to answer my question. "You probably know that nobody's ever done well for themselves by taking on an old line casino family like those people."

I shrugged. I remembered that Cody Masterson was Rachel's brother-in-law for a short time. Like Rachel, he had married into the Hannity clan, owners of an outdated Strip casino called The Outpost.

"I'm not too worried about that," I said. "If things don't work out, I have a pretty lucrative gig to fall back on."

Jeff gestured to my bikini, which was still clinging to my chest. "Speaking of which . . ."

I held up one finger. "So you think she can win?"

"Anything can happen," he said. "Look, if you're asking if I'm just stringing her along to get some billable hours, it's not like that. She hasn't even paid me yet, now that I think about it. With some new evidence, we can convince a jury that the guy did it, and that he owes your friend about fifty million bucks for killing her husband."

That was good enough for me. I leaned in to whisper in Jeff's ear. "Enough talk." I undid the Velcro on my bikini top. As usual, he watched me as though he'd never seen a naked woman before. I enjoyed that about Jeff, at least: his lust was unconditional.

Chapter 3

The next day I slept in until one and made myself a tuna melt, which was about the most complicated meal I ever allowed myself to prepare. My magazines were always prattling on about the need to add more fish to my diet, and I tried hard to ignore a nagging doubt that the combination of mayonnaise and cheddar cheese would counteract any health benefits coming from the tuna. I decided I didn't care.

With the morning officially shot, I decided to spend the afternoon enjoying the cool recirculated air in my condo and diving into the details of how the Cody Masterson murder case had played out in court. Apart from what Rachel and Jeff had told me, which was almost nothing, I remembered exactly two things about the case: Masterson was guilty as hell, and he was better looking than any man should be allowed to be. I had recently discovered that for twenty dollars a year, the Las Vegas *Review-Journal* lets you search and browse through old stories on its website, and I figured that would provide a good start. Too good, it turned out – my initial search for the name Cody Masterson turned up 189 hits, which was too much for me to read in this lifetime. I scrolled past several pre-murder society page stories and focused in on reports about the murder, Cody's indictment and the lead-up to trial.

There wasn't a lot to it. Three summers ago, George Hannity had been shot through the head at close range in what appeared to be a botched carjacking near a posh suburb ten miles east of downtown Las Vegas. All signs suggested that Hannity had been driving his convertible Mercedes SL-55 to his home when, at a deserted stoplight, someone pulled up, either in a car or on foot, and tried to wrest control of his car. Hannity was shot and killed, but the police speculated that something had spooked the carjacker and caused him to flee the scene without taking the Mercedes. No immediate suspects emerged, and the case looked destined to remain unsolved.

The murder of a young casino owner like George Hannity generated a slew of news stories, most of them under the byline of a writer named Leslie Trondheim. Her early reports focused on the increase in violent crime that had accompanied the area's rampant population growth in recent years. Other stories focused on the family tragedy: Hannity was only in his mid-thirties; had been married to Rachel (who was artfully described by the reporter as a "former entertainer") for three years; and he controlled thirty percent of an old, yet profitable, casino. All signs pointed to a long career as a wealthy businessman and community leader. One article mentioned him as part of a syndicate that was trying to bring a Major League Baseball franchise to town.

As I was scrolling through the stories, my computer flashed a warning that the website would log me out in another five minutes. I hadn't realized it, but I had been online for almost two hours. I was getting antsy, anyway. I was quickly learning that I wasn't cut out for this part of the job. I wanted to be on my feet and talking to people, not staring at a bunch of electrons on a screen in a lonely apartment. I logged out and pulled up the newspaper's public homepage, where I clicked on the contacts link.

I dialed the city desk number and the receptionist put me right through to Leslie Trondheim herself. She sounded polite but impatient. I introduced myself as a private investigator and asked whether she remembered working on the Masterson murder case.

"Of course," she said shortly. Stupid question. It was like asking Dan Rather if he remembered covering the Kennedy assassination.

"I wonder if you'd have a half hour sometime to talk about the case with me," I asked.

"Um hmm," she murmured. "Well, I'm on my way out the door right now, but maybe some time next week

I could give you that half hour." Next week was not going to do me any good. I thought for a moment.

"Could I buy you a drink tonight?" I asked. "Or dinner?" I'd read or heard somewhere that journalists are notorious cheapskates, and I hoped the offer of free food might do the trick.

She paused. I didn't know if she was really thinking about my offer, or if she just wanted me to think she was thinking about it. "That might work," she said coyly. "Your treat, you said?"

I smiled. "Naturally. You pick the place."

She thought for about four nanoseconds and said we'd meet up at Hugo's, a spot downtown near the newspaper's main offices. We agreed to meet there in an hour. On the way over, I wondered whether talking to a member of the media was such a great idea, but I decided I could probably learn more from her in an hour than I could from an entire week of reading through her old stories. Money and time well spent.

Hugo's Cellar is a joint famous with locals but all but unknown to the millions of visitors who pour into Las Vegas and never leave the area between the Strip and the airport. Hugo's caters to the kind of people who don't have any use for dancing fountains, wine stewards or martinis that have anything in them besides gin and vermouth.

For a Tuesday night, Hugo's was surprisingly crowded. The bar was on the left side of the entrance, and at it a large hunched woman was sitting by herself sipping a glass of pink wine. She was reading a worn paperback book through reading glasses that were attached to a chain around her neck.

"Ms. Trondheim?" I asked.

She twisted back to me and frowned—I was obviously not what she was expecting.

"Who in the world are you?" she asked.

"Raven. We just spoke on the . . ."

"The PI?" she practically spit out her pink wine. Her eyes dropped to my heels and made their way up to my chest, where they lingered a moment too long. "You're so…." She let the phrase hang in the air.

"Sorry," I said stupidly, not knowing what I was apologizing for. Who did she expect, Nancy Drew? I self-consciously adjusted my top to cover up some cleavage. It was mostly a waste of energy.

Leslie scooted the bar stool back a few inches and struggled a bit to get up. She stuck out her hand. "Call me Les," she said, and gave my hand a firm shake. She was all smiles and neck fat now. Apparently she had forgiven me.

"Are we eating or drinking?" I asked.

"Both," she said, and winked. She slurped down what looked like a half-glass of wine. So that's how it was. Les smiled apologetically and whispered something to the bartender. She stood only about five-two and looked like she ran a good two-hundred pounds, although instead of appearing wide and bulky she somehow carried the narrow, tubular frame of a juvenile walrus. A prominent quadruple chin gave her face a lumpy appearance, and it was framed by straight hair that used to be dark but was now streaked heavily with white and various shades of gray. With her reading glasses on, she could have passed for Benjamin Franklin.

I gestured toward the dining room and we made our way to a small table near the door. For some reason I pulled the chair out for her and helped her into the seat. She seemed to like that.

"You're a cute one," she said, looking me over as I sat down. I couldn't tell if she was being flirtatious or grandmotherly.

"Thanks." I hoped I wasn't blushing. A compliment was a compliment.

"So why in the world are you looking at that boring old case?" she asked, her eyes fixing on me over the reading glasses she still wore.

"Just idle curiosity, really."

She arched her left eyebrow up at me as though I'd just told the whopper of the century. Another glass of pink wine suddenly appeared in front of her, and I told the waiter to bring me a glass of prosecco, champagne's budget-friendly cousin.

"So how can I help?" She asked.

"Well, to put it bluntly," I said, "how the hell was Cody found not guilty?"

She smiled broadly. "Isn't it obvious? You have to remember that the jury had eight women on it, okay?" Her voice had the kind of rehearsed self-assurance shared by celebrities on talk shows who have answered the same few questions a million times. I hadn't known about the jury's heavily female slant, but I nodded anyway.

"And any woman would find it very difficult to send that man to prison. His face, his eyes . . ." She sighed dramatically, like a character in an Austen novel.

"Okay, okay," I laughed, cutting her off.

"It's true," she insisted. "No other explanation for it."

"So you think he was actually guilty?" My drink arrived. We had forgotten to study the menu, so we perused it quickly while the waiter stood by. Les ordered a lobster bisque to start and an entree of prime rib with a side of garlic potatoes. I got the bone-in rib eye with a house salad.

Les picked up where we'd left off. "I didn't say I thought he was guilty," she said carefully, "but I think any other man would probably have gone away for a long time. There was a lot of evidence, of course. When they find the murder weapon buried in your backyard, it's not a good thing. There was the motive to help his wife take over the casino. And Cody was known to not get along with George Hannity. And no one believed the alibi," she added confidently.

"The wife, you mean?" I vaguely recalled reading that Cody's wife Amy had backed up Cody's story that the two of them were in bed together the night of the murder.

She snorted softly. "Amy Masterson," she said, making a face. "Nice looking girl, but not on par with

Cody. Thinks she's a princess of some sort, I'm convinced. Let me tell you, though, she played well with the jury. She's as sweet as they come. Anyway, she did a number with that alibi. Cody took the stand first and said they were together the night of the murder. In bed. Then Amy comes on the stand and says, not only were they in bed together, they were making passionate love most of the night. She explained that her sweet husband was just too polite and gallant to mention those details to the jury."

I laughed. "Nice touch."

She continued. "And it helped that she was the victim's brother—no one would stick up for her own brother's killer, right? But I think she lied about the alibi business. Overall, Cody seemed pretty believable to me, but since I want to snuggle his brains out I might be a little biased," she admitted with a devilish smile.

I grinned. Leslie was not a shy woman to begin with, I figured, and the wine had her pretty well lubricated. I decided to let her take the conversation in whatever direction she wanted. "So what else?" I asked.

She paused to consider the question. "I've covered hundreds of trials, okay? And it's almost always an obvious case of guilt—a slam dunk or whatever man-invented metaphor you want to use." She slurped down a healthy glug of wine. "But this wasn't like that. There was a ton of evidence—the murder weapon being found in his backyard, for example—but it was like, why is this here, you know? Why kill a guy and clean the weapon of prints, but then bury the gun in your own backyard?"

"Hmm," I murmured. She had a point. "I'd at least drive it out to the desert or something."

"Right. Not exactly original, but it works. But I've seen so many of these cases that I'm always a little skeptical. And when you see these prosecutors and cops on a daily basis, you know they're not always the brightest bulbs."

"But Masterson wasn't really an Einstein himself, right?"

"Yeah. Look, I'm not saying he was innocent, just that it looked a little too neat to me."

That was the first time I'd heard anyone say that. It was pretty much common knowledge that Masterson was guilty, and the not-guilty verdict was always pointed to as a cautionary example of how high-priced lawyers could game the system to secure "justice" for the well-heeled.

The food came and we ordered another round of drinks. I decided I liked Leslie—she had grown wise and cautious through years of experience, I guessed, but rather than being bitter and jaded she seemed to process and dispense information with a sense of humor and a shrug. I was not surprised when she ordered dessert. By the time we parted ways, the wine had made Leslie more than a bit giddy. She thanked me profusely and joked I was the best date she'd had in years. Unfortunately for me, that sentiment was mutual.

Chapter 4

I had forgotten to close the shades the night before, and by 6:30 my bedroom was bathed in piercing sunlight. I knew it was too early to get up, but I couldn't get back to sleep. My mind was racing with thoughts of breakfast.

I needed to work off the pound of beef I'd eaten the night before, but I always felt uncomfortable using the building gym at this time of day. Okay, I hated using the gym at *any* time of day. It was full of motivated people who were burning carbs or toning thighs before heading off to their normal jobs as bankers or casino execs. I got most of my exercise dancing twenty hours per week, but that wasn't quite enough to keep my abs trim, and my thirty-something butt needed a little help if I wanted to compete for tips with eighteen-year-old girls who didn't know a porterhouse from a pancake. I knew if I thought about it another second, I'd find some way to rationalize being lazy, so I grudgingly put on my running clothes and headed out to the Strip.

At this hour the street itself was busy with morning traffic, but the wide sidewalks on either side of Las Vegas Boulevard were a ghost town. I ran past the scattered physical remains of the previous night's revelries: random call girl slips intermixed with assorted beer bottles, cigarette butts, and torn scraps of free newspapers advertising helicopter rides and Lake Mead cruises and Ferraris for rent. I encountered a few underage teens staggering about, sporting guilty grins and bleary eyes as they made a last brave stand before crashing. One kid gave me a double-take and then made a two-handed gesture and yelled something in Russian (I think) at me. A Catholic priest stood a lonely post collecting for charity, and a few casino workers emerged from buses and shuffled off to work. I reached the south end of the Strip at Mandalay Bay and headed back.

I returned to my condo feeling refreshed, and after watching a full hour of The View I figured I had procrastinated enough. It was time to do more homework: I needed to look at the court's file on the Masterson case. Although the court system made some filings available online, I knew their criminal cases were still only accessible in person at the clerk's dungeon of massive file cabinets. The kind of work I hated. Handling paper would probably give me paper cuts, I theorized, and my nighttime customers don't like it when their dancers are covered in band-aids.

I wanted a babysitter, so I picked up the phone. "Mike, I need to go downtown to the courthouse. Can you show me around?" Mike Caffrey was a private investigator who had the misfortune of being assigned as my supervising detective during my first year with a license. It meant he was supposed to supervise my work ten hours a month and certify to the licensing board that I wasn't a complete nut job. An observant Mormon, Mike seemed like a fish out of water in a town that deemed vice a virtue. I harbored a natural suspicion of people who didn't drink coffee or alcohol, but Mike had the tall, muscled body of an Iowa farmhand and his eyes were big and sapphire blue. And I had to respect the fact that he was a different breed from the skuzzy male clientele I dealt with most of the week.

He didn't sound enthusiastic about accompanying me downtown. "Haven't you been down there a lot already?"

"No," I lied. "I need someone to show me the ropes." I wasn't above using my helpless-woman voice.

"All right. But I have to testify at eleven-thirty."

"Fine. You at your office? I'll swing by and pick you up."

That was a relief. The prospect of facing piles of papers by myself gave me unpleasant flashbacks to college, not to mention the aforementioned danger of paper cuts. Mike would protect me.

I dialed downstairs, and they said my car would be waiting for me out front in five minutes. I sometimes felt guilty about spoiling myself with things like valet service, but I'd worked hard for a decade at a job most people found demeaning, and I figured I was due a little pampering. When I got down to the lobby, Tommy the valet (I didn't know his last name) was leaning on my car with a shy smile on his face. Vegas was full of beautiful people in the most unlikely places, and Tommy was one of them. He was probably twenty-two, but he looked sixteen. He didn't just have boyish good looks—he had jailbait good looks, especially in that tight gray valet uniform. We had been flirting outrageously for the better part of a year—well, *I* had been flirting—but he'd never taken the next step. Come to think of it, I don't think he'd ever said a single word to me. The story of my life. I spent my nights fending off the grabby hands of drooling, sex-crazed Neanderthals, but the guys I actually liked never made a move. Was that why I liked them in the first place?

Tommy opened the door on my silver Audi TT. I tried to give him an eyeful when I crouched into the driver's seat, but he was polite enough not to gawk. Damn him. He blushed and smiled widely at me like a trained chimp and shut the door without so much as a word. Oh well. At least I'd made him blush. I waved and headed out.

Mike's office was about ten blocks from the county courthouse. Downtown Las Vegas was experiencing something of a renaissance, but it was still a museum of 1960's architecture and buildings built primarily for function rather than form. That is the polite way of saying that Mike's office was dumpy. He met me at the street.

"This is your car?" He sounded a little offended.

I hadn't found occasion to tell Mike about my side job, and I didn't plan to. I figured it would be uncomfortable for the guy supervising me to learn that I probably earned five times what he did in a year, not to mention *how* I earned the money. He already seemed a little afraid of me, and I didn't want him offended by me as well.

"Just a little splurge," I said. "I got it to celebrate getting my PI's license."

"*Probationary* license," he corrected as he climbed in. Mike's idea of dressing for court meant a short-sleeved white shirt and a red tie, like a Bible salesman. The shirt looked cheap, but it showed off Mike's tanned, muscled arms. He was about the sexiest dork I'd ever met.

The Regional Justice Center is an imposing, all-business building completed early in this century at a time when the county actually had money. It's about twenty stories tall, brick and glass, and is made up of a number of rectangular boxes that make it look like a big city hospital. Mike led the way to the clerk's office on the third floor. When we arrived, the lobby was empty, and I approached a woman behind the glassed-in counter and requested the <u>State v. Masterson</u> file. The clerk, a middle-aged woman whose bold glasses made her look fashionable but not any younger, barely raised an eyebrow. She asked if I knew the case number, but then disappeared before I could answer. Apparently she knew exactly where the file was.

The file was not as mountainous as I feared. Mike pointed to a small table in the office lobby and we brought over the two file folders the clerk had given me. I knew they must have backup copies somewhere, but the clerk watched us surreptitiously to make sure we didn't run off with the file.

"So what kind of case are you working on?" Mike asked.

I pointed to the name on the file folder.

"State versus Masterson," he mouthed. Mike thought about it for a second and then pulled open the file. He dug out the criminal complaint and read the caption. "State of Nevada versus Cody A. Masterson. What exactly are you planning to do with this file?"

"I'm friends with Rachel Hannity, George Hannity's widow. She's asked me to take another look."

He folded his arms and bobbed his head seriously. "Uh huh. Take another look at what?"

"She's thinking about a civil case," I said nonchalantly. "Her lawyer thinks they can get a judgment if I can get a little more evidence."

"Wow." He sounded genuinely impressed. "That's kind of a big deal."

No shit it's a big deal, I thought.

We pawed through the binders in silence, like two teenagers on a study date. I wasn't looking for anything specific in the court's file, but my conversation with Les Trondheim had convinced me that I didn't know half of what I needed to know about the case. My half of the file contained pretty standard stuff, much of it in the form of pre-trial motions. In college I had spent most of a semester shadowing a criminal defense lawyer, and that was enough for me to forget law school forever. Despite what you see on TV, most legal work involves pushing papers around. The Masterson case didn't seem any different. There had been some motions about juror sequestration and suppressing evidence, but nothing too interesting.

The transcripts of the trial were more helpful. One officer described the gruesome crime scene, a stoplight intersection halfway between the city and George and Rachel's home in the suburbs. I hoped Rachel wasn't forced to listen to that line of gory testimony.

Mike cleared his throat. "The DA called your friend Rachel to the stand about half way through the trial, and Cody's lawyer made about a million objections along the way."

"Who was his lawyer?"

"Charlie Frank. He's …"

"I know who he is. He was the mob's lawyer, wasn't he?"

"One of the best," Mike said. He had me read a section of the transcript that looked pretty damning for Masterson. Rachel was on the stand testifying that her husband, like most people, would not pause at an intersection and roll down the window for a complete stranger in the middle of the night. The assailant had to be someone he knew, or at least recognized.

"Well," I said, "that kind of blows up the defense's whole car-jacking theory. George wasn't the sort of guy who would stop to chat with a stranger in the middle of the night."

"Nobody is."

Mike sat back in his chair and put his hands behind his head. "Add to that the gun found at his house, and the fact that killer had to be someone, like Cody, who Hannity knew. And there wasn't really another plausible theory to sell to the jury, either."

"Maybe I can quit right now," I said, only half-joking.

"I wouldn't. You only get one chance at a civil trial, and you don't want to go in unless you've got something rock solid."

Maybe Mike wasn't as dumb as he seemed.

I had read enough of the transcript, and I knew I would have voted to convict Cody Masterson. It was 11:15, and Mike excused himself to leave for court. I thanked him and flashed a big smile. He didn't blush.

Chapter 5

I grabbed a drive-thru salad and scarfed it down during the ninety-five red lights I hit on my way home. As I sat in traffic, I was thinking there were only two conceivable forms of hard evidence I could dig up to contradict Cody's story. If a witness had seen the murder and could be convinced to come forward, that could wrap the case up nicely. I wasn't holding out hope for a witness, though. The murder was committed at a deserted intersection in the suburbs after midnight, and the cops had spent weeks canvassing for witnesses. No one had come forward in the three years since then.

Instead, it seemed the best available route would be to find evidence that would undermine Cody's alibi. For that, I needed to talk to people who actually knew

Cody and his wife—people at the casino they owned. I left a message on Rachel's cell phone. Although she was on the outs with the people running the casino now, she might have some ideas on which people inside the casino could be trusted. I didn't want to barge in there like a bull in a china shop asking pointed questions about the owners and their pals.

When I got home, I poured myself a Diet Coke and put on an old Metropolitan Opera LP of *La Bohème*. Last year I inherited a few boxes of classical and opera albums from my maternal grandmother, and was surprised to find that a lot of companies still sold turntables. Some people even claimed that vinyl produced a richer sound, but my ear wasn't expert enough to notice.

With a young Pavarotti for company, I forced myself to buckle down and do some more homework. As a privately owned casino, the Outpost didn't have to file public securities reports or hold meetings with stockholders. But, being a casino, it did have to make the filings required by Nevada's Gaming Control Board. According to the Control Board's online records, Cody Masterson was the Outpost's president and chief executive officer. Amy Masterson, his wife, was listed as the chairman of the board, and the directors of the company comprised, not surprisingly, the two Mastersons, plus the general counsel and corporate secretary, a woman named Laura Clavette. The general manager and chief operating officer was a man named Philip d'Angelo. Apparently it took a lot of fancy titles to run a glorified gambling hall. I figured that all of these people had a vested interest in not telling me anything—they were all, in some way, dependent on Cody's staying out of trouble.

Rachel called me back around four o'clock.

"You have to understand, Raven, that I haven't been in contact with those people since George died. He was my only connection."

"I was thinking, though, that I'd have to get in there somehow and talk to people close to Cody. Don't you think the prospect of financial gain would get somebody to talk?" I asked.

"You mean like a reward?"

"Kind of. After all, a hundred thousand here or there will be pocket change if we win a lawsuit."

"I guess that's okay." Rachel sounded skeptical.

"But we have to be a little bit tricky about it. If we just want the information, that's one thing. But if we want it to hold up in court, you don't want the defense to be able to say the witness was bribed," I said. "It kind of hurts their credibility if the defense counsel can get them to admit they have a financial stake in saying that Cody is guilty."

"Good point," she replied. I thought she sounded a tiny bit impressed. "The problem is that Cody doesn't usually associate with the staff very much. He sees himself as above most of them, even though just a few years ago he was just a stage dancer like me."

"He was?"

"Oh *yeah*," she laughed, apparently unphased by my ignorance. "I forget the name of the show, but it was one of those all-male revues with a cheesy name, and it played a few years at the Tropicana." She warmed to the topic, her voice filled with amusement.

"Cody came in from Tahoe with his long blond hair and stole the show pretty quickly. They had a routine where he would go around the audience and lasso a woman and bring her up on stage and do all sorts of suggestive things involving the woman and the rope. It drove the women wild—myself included. They screamed like they do for Justin Bieber. Anyway, Amy Hannity saw the show, asked to meet him, and a few months later she became Amy Masterson."

"Wow. So both Hannity kids married people who took their clothes off for a living. George married you, and Amy married Cody."

"Yeah, their parents were *pissed*."

"Anyway, I was looking at the forms they filed with the Gambling Board, and it seems a guy named Philip d'Angelo is the highest-ranking officer with no ties to the family. Is that right?"

Rachel sighed. "Unfortunately. He wouldn't have been my choice to run the place, which is what he basically does."

"Not your kind of guy?" I prodded.

"Phil's not anyone's kind of guy," she chuckled. "Big chip on his shoulder. He rose up through the ranks. Not exactly from the mail room, but almost. He was a dealer, pit boss, floor manager, and worked security before he took over day-to-day operations. Great manager, though, and efficient. He's a driven guy, ambitious as *hell*. And he's one of the few people Cody and Amy seem to trust. Anyway, I wouldn't hesitate to make contact with him, but be discreet about it."

"Of course," I replied. Although as a general rule I found it hard to be discreet with anyone.

"Frankly I don't know him well enough to know if he's blindly loyal to the Mastersons or whether he might cooperate. It's worth a shot, though."

"Assuming he knows anything," I added. "Anyone else I might try?"

"Not that I can think of. Like I said, I'm kind of out of the loop at this point. Good luck."

I hung up with Rachel and couldn't find any reason to put off talking to Phil d'Angelo, the man in charge at the Outpost. I called down to the valet to get my car and found my way north up the Strip. Normally I might have walked the mile and a half, but I'd just showered and the afternoon heat was intense. It was about 4:30 and the rush hour traffic was in its full glory, made worse by the fact that the faux volcano in front of the Mirage was hissing violently and shooting flames twenty feet into the air. At that hour, all it took was one rental car full of gawking tourists to bring traffic to a virtual standstill.

I reached the Outpost and reluctantly let a skuzzy looking valet park my Audi. The casino was appropriately named. It had actually been something of an outpost in earlier days, an isolated oasis between the Strip hotels to the south and the downtown area to the north. Now it stood out as an eyesore, as out of place as a pawn shop on Madison Avenue. The glistening, billion-dollar resorts that surrounded the hotel on both sides had Bentleys and Jaguars clogging their valet lanes, while the Outpost had a single valet line and nothing more fancy than a Buick parked out front. I felt sorry for my little Audi.

As I entered through the main doors, I was greeted immediately with the telltale clangs of nickels hitting tin and a chorus of bells and computerized music riffs emanating from the slot machines. Most of the more modern casinos had some sort of theme or motif to them, but the Outpost didn't have a theme unless you counted second-hand smoke.

I made my way to the small hotel lobby just off the casino floor. The three check-in lines were jammed, so I scanned the lobby for anyone who could save me some time. I zeroed-in on a woman, about twenty-five, who stood shuffling papers and clicking away on her computer behind the check-in desk. She was surprisingly attractive. Good looking women were a dime a dozen in Las Vegas, but they didn't usually pursue their calling behind the desks at rundown hotels. Her window was marked CLOSED, and she didn't look like she was in the mood to be bothered.

She seemed to have a sixth sense for anyone who might dare interrupt her work. "I'm sorry, I'm not open," she said, not taking her eyes from her small computer screen. Her red name tag said her name was Linda.

"Oh, I'm sorry," I said, "I'm here to see Mr. d'Angelo. I'm an old friend."

She finally looked up from her screen and paused. "Um, I don't think he's in right now. I can check for you if you give me two minutes, okay?" She shot me a very winning smile, probably thinking I was the head honcho's daily call girl.

"Of course." After three or four minutes, she left her post and disappeared into a back room. I used the opportunity to catch a nicotine buzz off of the lingering smoke cloud. When Linda returned, she told me with overstated sadness that Mr. d'Angelo was not presently in, but if I left my name she would make sure he knew I stopped in.

"No thanks," I said. "I'll just try to catch him another time." I knew my name would mean nothing to d'Angelo by itself, and I didn't feel like leaving my business card and announcing to the whole casino that a private investigator had stopped by.

As usual, my decision to have a healthy salad for lunch was backfiring. I had become ravenous for real food involving meat and cheese, so I wandered out of the lobby and decided to brave the casino café for a little snack. The Outpost's restaurant was as utilitarian as they come. The goal, evidently, was to satisfy the appetites of gamblers as quickly as possible so they would return to their tables or slot machines without any needless delay. I sat at the counter by myself and ordered a beer and a cheeseburger. The beer arrived in about twenty seconds and the burger followed not too long after. Two bites in, I heard the swivel chair next to me squeak as someone sat down.

"Always nice to see an old friend," the stranger remarked. Since I'd been attacking my cheeseburger with the single-mindedness of a frenzied shark, I was forced to finish chewing and gulp a slug of beer before turning to address the stranger on my right. He was lean and tanned, with a full head of black hair and a face lined by a combination of sun exposure and—I took a wild guess—second-hand smoke. His dark eyes peered into me, and I thought I detected a faint smile, as though he enjoyed catching me off-guard and in the middle of a bite.

"Uh," I coughed. "I'm guessing you're Mr. d'Angelo," I said lamely. Linda must have pointed me out to him.

"You must be a detective," the man quipped sarcastically. His eyes became lighter, even more amused than before.

"Actually, I am." I needed another slug of beer to clear my throat. His eyes shot up in surprise, and he looked me over without a hint of self-consciousness. "Well, if this is about that red light I ran in 2003, I confess. Take me away, officer!" He thought he was pretty funny.

"No, I'm a *private* investigator." I gave a polite chuckle. "Raven McShane's the name." I offered my hand, and he shook it.

"Phew!" he exclaimed in mock relief. "Call me Phil. How can I help you? Does my ex-wife think I'm making more money than I claim?"

"Not quite. I'm actually here about casino business." I looked around, trying to appear casual. The guy behind the bar was pretending not to listen. "I guess I shouldn't beat around the bush," I said softly. "What I'm really interested in is Cody Masterson's past brush with the law."

"What does that have to do with anything?" Phil asked.

"Well, obviously he was found not guilty, but a lot of people were surprised by that verdict."

"I'm surprised every morning when I wake up alive," Phil said, shrugging. He narrowed his eyes and sized me up. "Look, I don't know what your angle is, but I think I see what you're getting at," he said, standing up. "You want me to betray my boss and I'm not going to."

"Fair enough." After a few brief questions, he had guessed my angle and wanted nothing to do with me. "Loyalty is a rare thing these days," I said.

Phil thought for a second. "Yes it is, but the Hannitys have always treated me right, and I don't see any reason to help you out," he explained. "No offense."

"No, I understand. Thanks for stopping by."

"Enjoy your burger," he said curtly as he stood up. He took a last look down my shirt. "By the way," he said, "you'd probably make more money as a cocktail waitress than a two-bit private eye or whatever you are." He turned and walked away. Rachel was right: this guy was an asshole.

Chapter 6

I was trying to think of a Plan B when someone brushed me on the shoulder. I thought maybe d'Angelo had returned to take another swipe at me, but it wasn't Phil. This man was paler and much thicker through the neck. He was younger than Phil, probably forty, although his hair was nearly all white. His face was pink and pockmarked, and he wore a name tag that read "E. Holman" above the word "SECURITY." He was looking at me as though he knew me. I offered a generic smile, but he didn't smile back. I soon sensed another presence looming behind me, a presence that wore a particularly objectionable brand of cologne. The presence gave me an unfriendly tap on my right shoulder.

"We'd like you to come with us," said the surprisingly soft, husky voice behind me. I was still facing the white-haired man on my right and had to crane my neck to face the voice. The speaker was a much taller man of athletic build with dark brown hair and a mustache. He wore a black dress shirt underneath a gray sport coat. No name tag. He looked a little like the man who used to be on the Brawny paper towel packages, but he didn't seem to share the Brawny man's warm and fuzzy outlook on life.

"Um," I stuttered, standing up fully. "No thanks. Just finishing my beer." I pointed lamely to my half-finished mug.

"It won't take long. Please, miss," Holman said, gesturing with his hand. He was polite but insistent.

The Brawny man's hand came down on my shoulder, and I found myself being scooted away from my seat.

"Okay. But I'm meeting my boyfriend in a few minutes," I lied, "so I don't have long."

The white-haired Holman grunted. Instead of walking me back through the casino, the two led me through a small door next to the bar that I hadn't noticed before. I was beginning to get a twinge of nervousness, but I hadn't done anything wrong. I figured either Phil d'Angelo wanted to see me in the privacy of his office or these guys had me confused with some two-bit card counter. Or they thought I was a hooker.

If the Outpost's public face was somewhat tarnished and trashy, behind closed doors the place looked like a fleabag motel that hadn't seen any maintenance since the Carter Administration. The hallway they led me down was dimly lit by unattractive rectangular wall sconces, but even the dim lighting couldn't hide the stained linoleum floor that creaked under our weight. They ushered me into a small room furnished only by a small square table and two plastic chairs that looked like they were lifted from a Soviet dentist's office. It smelled like an old Catholic school gym. A fluorescent light buzzed and flickered overhead.

The three of us stood in the small room in awkwardly close proximity. I could smell the cheap cologne wafting off of the Brawny man to my right, and Holman stood directly in front of me underneath the light, which cast an eerie halo over his features. He offered a pained smile and held up his hands as if to say everything was all right.

"Our boss sent us down here to make sure you understood how things stand. He wasn't sure he conveyed his message clearly enough."

"No, I got it," I said. "Just a little personal matter between me and him."

"That's where we might have a little disagreement," Holman said, enunciating his words carefully. "You see, our boss explained what it is you wanted to talk about, and that's something that could affect all of us." He let the vague but pregnant statement hang in the air. At this point the big man put his hand on my shoulder and pressed me down into the seat. The two goons loomed menacingly over me.

"I see," was all I could muster. I could feel my stomach doing cartwheels, and my mind raced to catch up with the situation. I hadn't considered the possibility that d'Angelo would share our little visit with his staff. Nor had I considered the possibility that the staff wouldn't be too keen on me upsetting the applecart. Apparently an entire business could have a vested interest in keeping a murderer out of jail.

"So you appreciate our position, then?" Holman asked softly. He wore a muffled smirk that would have produced a more violent response from me if I hadn't been outnumbered.

"I guess I do," I said meekly, even though he hadn't explained what their so-called position was. It didn't take a degree in communications to get his meaning, though. "I will definitely keep that in mind," I added, beginning to stand up. This time Holman touched me gently on the shoulder before I was fully upright.

"Just so there is no confusion," he said, "you are not to enter this property ever again." His tone reeked of contempt.

"Not a problem," I said, trying my best to appear cool. "I'll just show myself out." Both of them nodded, but Holman's hand was still on my shoulder. He eased up for a second, but then he began digging his fingers into the tendons at the base of my neck. I could feel his stubby fingernails and the hardened calluses on the tips of his fingers as he pressed into my bare skin. It hurt like a bitch.

I squirmed out of his grasp and stood up. They were loving this, both of them standing there grinning like high school jocks. Big on intimidation, short on brains. I had an idea. I got close to Holman. Real close. My chest was pressing against the front of his shirt, as though we were dancing to a slow tune. I tried to put a sorrowful, apologetic look on my face. I made my lips pouty and looked up into his eyes. He looked confused, but interested. But mostly he looked idiotic.

"I'm sorry," I pouted. I brought my left hand up and slowly ran my finger across his chest. I slid two fingers between the buttons on the front of Holman's cheap dress shirt, and then I executed my rudimentary plan. When you're an exotic dancer for ten years, you develop certain muscles below the waist that have no business being on any honest woman's body. I could climb a dancing pole without using my hands. In a pinch, I could crack a walnut between my thighs. And with a little practice, I could probably kick a field goal from fifty yards. Maybe it wasn't a fair fight, but I did what any other woman would do. I grasped Holman's shirt tightly, for support, and with all my force I whipped my right knee up between his legs. It was a full Rockette kick, except that his scrotum got in the way. Oops.

He shrieked in pain for a second and then began wailing a silent scream that only dogs could hear. As he slumped over the table in agony I pushed past them and got the hell out of there. I retraced my steps down the hallway and emerged next to the bar and did a quick glance down at my shirt. I was wearing a thin gray t-shirt that was now half-soaked with sweat. I held my arms against my sides to hide the sweat, moving towards the valet stand in a fast waddle like a penguin trying to escape a polar bear. I figured I was safe as long as I was out in the open. Cameras were watching everything, and there were at least fifty people lingering around.

My heart was still pounding. I couldn't believe I had just been back-roomed. That was something they did in the days of the Rat Pack and Bugsy Siegel, not in the twenty-first century Disney version of Las Vegas that I lived in. Thankfully, my car arrived quickly. The inbred valet flashed a lascivious and mirthless smile at me while I got into the car. Did this lowlife think he was getting a tip? I thought he could use a knee to the groin, too, but I just flipped him off and gunned the engine.

Somehow I made it back to my apartment without incident. The familiarity of my condo was reassuring, and I checked myself in the mirror. My neck was red where Holman had dug his claws into me, and my knee had a nasty bruise forming. I must have bashed it against a chair when I bolted out of that back room.

It wasn't even six o'clock, but I didn't feel like working or doing much of anything else. I decided to give myself the evening off and clunked out on the couch halfway through an old Steve Martin movie.

Chapter 7

Friday morning I woke up on the couch with a throbbing headache. Remarkably, I'd slept right through the night without any nightmares about the assholes at the Outpost. I'd left the TV on, and was now treated to a children's cartoon featuring a pair of disturbingly well-endowed female superheroes. Their chirpy voices stabbed like daggers in my head. It was definitely a three-Advil morning.

I forced myself out of bed and plopped down at my computer, where I found an email from an Indiana woman named Barbara Finley. She wanted to hire me to keep tabs on her husband while he was in town for a bachelor party. He'd said he was going to Florida on a golf trip, but she had learned otherwise. I emailed her back with a copy of my standard retainer agreement.

Most people seemed put off by the high rates I charged, so I didn't expect to hear back from her.

After getting myself together, I realized I needed to talk to Rachel again. Getting banned from the Outpost was more than a minor setback. It was obvious that Phil d'Angelo wasn't going to play nice, and it seemed likely that he'd already turned the entire casino staff against me. I would need a whole different approach to the case or Rachel would have to find someone else.

I left a message on Rachel's cell phone asking if she had any other ideas as to Outpost people I could talk to. I plopped back on the couch, hoping my headache would go away. After a half-hour of mindless television and about three quarts of water, it went from a throbbing pain to a dull ache. I considered that a minor victory.

After lunch I decided to give Mike a call—he'd find the story about the Outpost amusing, at the very least. I reached him on his cell. He had a pleasant sounding laugh, but I was determined to take offense anyway.

"I didn't find it that funny. A little dramatic of them, don't you think?"

"What, the treatment?"

"If that's what you call it."

"You haven't been doing this very long. Even the big corporate hotels have back rooms. They can legally detain you if they think a crime's been committed," he explained.

"And if they don't think any crime has been committed?" I pressed.

"They just say 'oops'".

"Somehow I don't think the Bellagio has goons hauling people to back rooms and digging into people's flesh," I said.

"You never know. I've heard some scary things about people who take out six figure markers and try to skip out when they lose."

I wasn't really buying it. I told Mike I was going to hole up indoors for the rest of the day, and I spent the afternoon surfing the web for information about Cody Masterson and feeling like the world's worst private investigator.

Around five o'clock my agent called to remind me I had a three-hour engagement the next morning at a tire convention. Conventions were annoying, but they were easy gigs: wander around, hand out a few hundred pamphlets for shock absorbers or dental tape, laugh at a few dozen bad jokes, and pocket a check for $1,500. Conventions were hugely preferable to stuffy VIP cocktail parties, where I was expected to mingle and feign interest in the latest developments in laser orthodontics (this week) or wheelchair equipment (next month). And convention work gave me a cover job whenever my family started nosing around about how I made my money.

After dinner I managed to get to Cougar's to dance for a few hours. I borrowed some cream from one of the girls to cover up Holman's fingernail marks on my shoulder, but my heart wasn't in the performance. With my convention starting at ten the next morning, I decided to attend to my three regulars who were partying Friday night and called it an evening by midnight.

The convention at the Bellagio was uneventful except for the ice cream cone that got spilled on my shoulder. The ice cream was chocolate, and my Yves St. Laurent suit was vanilla. Luckily the vendor who spilled it was horrified and cut me a check on the spot for my dry cleaning bill. I felt ridiculous for about an hour, but it proved to be a great conversation starter for the men at the convention.

Rachel called me back around 2:00 on Saturday. I got straight to the point.

"It was bound to happen eventually," she said nonchalantly. "Even a ratty little place like the Outpost keeps a close watch on who comes and goes. Even if Phil was going to talk, they wouldn't like you nosing around there too much."

"I suppose," I said. "But that kind of cramps my style. If I can't get back in there to talk to anybody, it'll be hard to dig much deeper."

She paused. "That's true. Even if no one who works there now will talk to you, that doesn't mean we're screwed. Let me think about it and get back to you, okay?"

Rachel left me a message while I was in the shower, asking me to get in touch with a man named Mel Block, who she said was the Outpost's general manager before Phil d'Angelo took over. The Mastersons had wanted new blood after George died, and Mel had seemed more than happy to retire to San Diego. Rachel said Mel was one of the few people at the casino who'd been nice to her, but they had lost track of each other in the last few years.

I tried the number Rachel had given me for Mel Block, but there was neither an answer nor an answering machine. I tried calling again twice more that afternoon with the same result. I made an early stir fry dinner and headed over to Cougar's. Saturday nights were the most profitable of the week (Friday was second), and I expected four or five regulars to pay me a visit. I found six, plus a cute young German poker player who I'd danced for the night before. A regular in the making, I hoped.

I woke Sunday just before noon. My first thought was that I really had no leads to go on, even after almost a week working on the case. It was not just frustrating, it was embarrassing. I called Mel Block's number in San Diego again with no luck. After putzing around my apartment for an hour I found myself on my balcony with a stack of Shape and Cosmopolitan magazines that had been building up since May. A can of cheddar Pringles somehow found its way into my lap.

My phone rang around two o'clock.

"Raven, this is Sean Whelan with LVPD. Returning your call from the other day."

I was silent for what felt like a full minute, my brain full of cobwebs. "Hi Lieutenant, thanks for getting back to me." I had completely forgotten that I'd phoned him on Tuesday.

"Sorry it's taken so long. Rough week. Actually I thought I'd get your machine," he said. "Working on a Sunday, huh?" He was trying to be friendly, but it came off as hollow.

"Nope, I'm not really working. It's my cell number. I was just wondering if I could talk with you for a few minutes about the Masterson murder case. You were in charge of the investigation, right?"

"Wow, that's an oldie but goodie. Yeah, I was the lead detective on that one. Your message was kind of cryptic. What exactly can I help you with?"

Whelan's call had caught me off-guard, and I wasn't prepared with anything useful to ask him. "I wonder if I could come to your office or something," I suggested. "Are you in tomorrow?"

"We can't do this on the phone? I'm a little busy." He suddenly sounded snippy.

"Sure, just give me . . ."

"Sorry," he interrupted. "Like I said, rough week. My wife left me, actually. Took the kids to her mom's place up in Oregon. Kind of sudden. I've been out the last two days and I'm just trying to catch up."

"God, that's awful," I said, not knowing how else to respond. We were both silent for a minute. My mind went into overdrive. "Lieutenant, I'm going out on a limb here, but your name is Irish, right?"

"Yeah. I'm a thoroughbred, actually. Why?"

"Well, I'm half Irish myself. It sounds like you could use a pint of Guinness. Or two. We can talk about Cody Masterson and I'll buy you a couple."

He was quiet for a few seconds. "What the hell, okay," he laughed. "I know, what are the odds, right? I'm Irish *and* I drink." His voice sounded a little lighter.

"We can toast the old country." Like Whelan said, what the hell.

"I don't give a shit what we toast, but I'm gonna take you up on your offer. I really don't think you have any idea what you've gotten yourself into," he said, laughing. We agreed to meet at seven at an Irish pub about ten minutes from the Strip. I'd never been there before, but Sean recommended it enthusiastically.

Before I left I finished off some leftover Chinese food and tried calling Mel Block in San Diego, again without luck. I figured Block could be on vacation. It was July, after all, and he might have a summer place or something. But at least there should be an answering machine, I thought. Or maybe I just had the wrong number.

O'Callaghan's Irish Pub & Grille looked kitschy and formulaic from the outside, as if someone had assembled the place from a build-your-own Irish Pub kit. On the inside, though, it was surprisingly homey and comfortable. If anything, the Irish pub theme was understated. Lieutenant Whelan was sitting by himself at the corner of a large square bar, perched with a good view of the Yankees-Indians game on ESPN. He was bulkier than I'd thought, but I recognized him from the description he'd given me: red faced with a curly mess of yellowish white hair. By the time I sat down, he'd already done some damage to a tall glass of stout. I wondered if it was his first.

He looked like he hadn't slept well, with bags hanging from his eyes and a pronounced slump to his frame. Or maybe he'd just gone on a three-day bender. We made our introductions and I ordered a Guinness of my own. Whelan wasn't shy about looking me over. I was dressed pretty conservatively, with a short-sleeved white oxford shirt buttoned up most of the way and a pair of thin beige linen shorts. Pink sandals were the only interesting thing I was wearing.

"I have to say," he said, "you're not what I was expecting."

"Is that a compliment?"

"I think so. Is it still legal in this country to pay a woman a compliment? Or is that some kind of harassment or something?"

I smiled. "I've got a pretty thick skin. You can compliment me all you want."

"That's good." He looked around. "You're really a detective?"

I nodded.

"Sorry," he said. "With my wife splitting this week, I'm just paranoid some sleazebag lawyer is trying to get pictures of me with a younger woman."

I didn't feel comfortable getting so personal with a guy I'd just met, so I dove in to the purpose of our visit. "I've been hired to take another look at the Masterson case," I explained. "Basically, my client wants enough evidence to take the case before a civil jury."

"Wow." He whistled for effect and thought about it for a minute. "You work for Mrs. Hannity?"

"Yes. She's a friend of mine. I'm wondering what your thoughts about the verdict were, and whether there was much in the way of evidence you had that didn't make it into the trial."

"She looks a lot like you, actually. Except that she's blonde, of course."

I nodded. He was still on the looks thing. I didn't feel it appropriate to mention that my boobs were bigger than Rachel's.

"Fair enough," he said, picking up on my silent impatience. He drained his beer and signaled to the bartender. "Couple of Irish car bombs for my friend and me." He turned to me and grinned. "Guinness ain't working fast enough," he whispered conspiratorially.

The waiter brought over two foaming pints of Guinness and a pair of shot glasses. He poured a half-inch of Bailey's Irish Cream in each shot glass and topped them off with Jameson whiskey. He waited a few seconds while the head on the Guinness settled, and then he dropped the shot glasses into the beers.

"Chug," Whelan said, pushing one of the glasses over to me. We both chugged for what felt like a full two minutes, and both of us wound up wearing brown foamy mustaches.

"Wow," I said, impressed. "Where has that drink been all my life?"

Whelan seemed pleased. "They're big with the guys in the fire department. I kind of stole that one from them awhile ago." He signaled the bartender again and turned to me. "If you don't mind, I'm going to let you buy me some plain old whiskey. My bladder isn't what it used to be," he confided under his breath. I told him I'd gladly join him in a couple double Jameson's on the rocks. It was my dad's old drink.

Whelan was a little overweight, but not exactly fat. He looked about fifty-five—old for a cop—but had a full mop of hair. I wasn't sure how long he'd been sitting at the bar before I got there, but the man seemed like he could hold his liquor and knew what he was doing. I hoped he did, because my stomach was getting nervous about the prospect of drinking whiskey on top of a pint of beer. On top of two-day-old Chinese food.

"So you want to know about Cody Masterson," he said, and took a long swig of Jameson's. "I still think about that case, do you believe that? Everyone's got a white whale, I guess, but that one still nags at me."

"How come?"

"Well, let me put it this way. If you're looking for more evidence, you're not gonna find any. We gave it everything we had, and the jerk still got off."

"I was kind of afraid of that," I said. "So you're convinced he did it?"

He paused, studying the ice cubes melting in his drink. "I'm convinced he should have been convicted," he said. "Whether he actually did it or not, that's another question." He looked at me and smiled. "How's that for my impersonation of a lawyer?"

"Not bad, except for the fact that you don't have horns. So what was Cody like in the interrogation room?"

"Cool. Never cracked. Personally I think he'd been very well coached, but one of my guys actually believed him. Remember, he had Charlie Frank representing him. The man is a snake, but if the shit ever hit the fan for me, he'd be the first guy I'd call."

"That's about the best compliment a lawyer could ever expect to receive," I said. "So why aren't you completely sure about Masterson?"

He sighed and waved the bartender over for another round. I was still nursing mine, but he'd polished his whiskey off like it was sweet tea. I began wondering what his plan was for getting home, or if cops simply didn't worry about DUI's.

"I'm set to retire in another year, full pension. Although if my wife makes it official and divorces me, I'll be working 'til I die. Anyway, the point being I don't give a shit like I used to."

The bartender poured him another double and I put a hand over my glass to signal I was fine. "What bothered me about that case was how the ball got rolling in the first place. You know, we were all set to call it a random street killing, a carjacking, until we got an anonymous tip to search Masterson's backyard."

I nodded. "Where you found the gun."

"Yeah. We found that thing buried back there, no prints. It was either wiped down or the killer used gloves. The point is, either someone knew Cody did it and knew where the weapon was, or someone planted the gun in his yard to frame him. We went with the first option."

"Occam's Razor," I said. "Usually the simplest explanation is the right one," I said. I pulled that one out of my ass.

Whelan's eyes got big. "Wow. Beautiful *and* smart."

I twirled my hair playfully and grinned. "So no one ever suggested someone was trying to set Cody up, right?"

"Exactly. Well, they had to come up with something, but it was pretty vague. How else do you explain the murder weapon being buried in your yard if you didn't do it?"

The beer and whiskey were affecting my brain a little bit, but I was still able to process what Whelan was saying. I couldn't help thinking that it was surprisingly similar to what Les Trondheim had told me. These were the people most intimately familiar with the case, and none of them was as convinced of Cody's guilt as the man on the street seemed to be. If these people weren't certain, it was beginning to make sense that a jury of twelve didn't find him guilty beyond a reasonable doubt. On the other hand, lawyers, cops and journalists were trained to be skeptics. Sometimes the conventional wisdom was right because it was based on common sense.

"Well, I guess it doesn't look promising for me," I said.

"Sorry, I don't know what else to tell you."

We sat in silence for a minute, our eyes fixed on the baseball game. I checked my watch discreetly. It was only 7:45. That meant we'd polished off a night's worth of booze in less than an hour, and Whelan seemed only to be hitting his stride. I expected if I left him alone he'd stay by himself for five or six more whiskeys. He hadn't opened up about his marital troubles at all, but it seemed like the man could use some company—and maybe something to distract him from his problems on the home front.

I didn't feel like sucking back more drinks and then having to call a cab home, and I wasn't about to ask Whelan if he wanted to go out for chocolate malts or ice cream sodas. The idea came to me in a flash.

Whelan drained his Jameson and replaced the glass on the bar extremely delicately, as though performing a part of some intricate Japanese tea ceremony. He was starting to seem a bit drunk. "Easy there, big fella," I said. "Hey, my friend dances at Cougar's, and I was going to head over there to catch her on stage. You in?" It seemed the perfect way to distract this horny Irishman.

Whelan gaped at me as though I had been speaking Swahili, but his expression was a mixture of confusion and interest. He looked perfectly sober except for the slightest tinge of pink in his eyes. Over the years I'd learned that although lots of men weren't the strip club "type," very few men actually said no when the opportunity arose. Whelan did not disappoint. "You shitting me?" he asked.

"Nope, let's go. I'll get a cab."

"You sure? I don't want to horn in on your social scene or anything."

"You'd be doing me a favor," I said. "I'll feel like a weirdo if I go by myself."

"Sold," he said.

We got our things together and I left a pile of cash on the bar. After our cab dropped us off, we shared a quick drink and then I handed Whelan off to one of the most popular dancers working that night. When she led him away to the back room, Whelan looked like he'd just won the lottery. If anyone could take Whelan's mind off his troubles, it was Shayla.

Chapter 8

I was getting antsy. A whole week spent on a single case was a record for me, and I had almost nothing to show for it. Last night Lieutenant Whelan had pretty much confirmed what I already knew, which was that Cody Masterson was probably, but not definitely, guilty of the crime but that there was no other magic evidence lurking out there that could help Rachel win her civil case.

Mel Block, the former general manager at the Outpost who Rachel had said I should call, was about the only person in the world I hadn't talked to about this case. He was getting on my nerves. In this day and age, who doesn't have an answering machine or voicemail? I even Googled him. A blank. It was time to pay him a personal visit. I picked up the phone.

"Mike, it's too hot here. You've got to come with me to San Diego." It was totally out of left field, but I thought it was worth a shot.

Silence.

"It's for this case I'm working on. You can bill the time to my client. And just think, you'd get your ten hours of supervising me done with all at once."

Nothing.

"Hello?"

"Still here."

"Well?"

"I have a report I need to get done today."

"I'll drive. Bring your laptop and write it in the car."

"No," he said. There was a pause, and then an opening. "Where would we stay?"

"I don't know, maybe a youth hostel?"

"A youth hostel."

"A little joke. I'll find something nice. Go home, pack for a night, and I'll pick you up there. The client has deep pockets." I didn't tell him that the client also had *empty* pockets.

"You don't know where I live."

"I'm a detective, remember?"

"Strange how I forget that sometimes."

"See you at noon." What was he so afraid of? I didn't bite. Hard.

That gave me all of an hour and a half to get ready and find a hotel online. We were only going for the night and I wouldn't need to pack much. Packing for San Diego was easy: shorts, tank top, unmentionables, sandals, sun screen. The hotel was easy, too. According to the hotel's website, it had a pool on the roof. And there was a shopping mall two blocks away in case we needed anything else.

I headed out of my building onto Russell Road and then hopped onto I-15 heading south towards Mike's house. He was waiting for me out front of a nice ranch house with a palm tree next to the driveway. Nothing fancy, but it wasn't a rat hole either. Mike had ditched the Willy Loman look in favor of a fitted brown t-shirt, khaki shorts and sandals. A gray backpack was slung over his left shoulder. With his sunglasses on, he looked like a model in a sporting goods catalog. A definite improvement. He threw his bag in the back seat and got in the car.

"Thanks," he said.

"What for?"

"I need to get out of here. I haven't left town in months."

"Buckle up," I said. I patted him on the thigh. It had the approximate firmness of titanium. "Jesus, where do you work out?"

He shifted uncomfortably in his seat. "Got a gym in the basement," he mumbled.

I turned and smiled at him. He was blushing.

Mike clicked away on his computer for most of the ride. He seemed to have steady work chasing after deadbeats and casino cheats, but it didn't seem very lucrative. Or exciting. After stopping for a light lunch, we hit the outskirts of L.A. a little after 2:00 and then veered south towards San Diego. I had only been to California a handful of times in my life, but somehow the names of the cities on the exits we passed had a familiar ring: San Bernardino, Riverside, Temecula, Escondido. I pulled out the map and had Mike guide me to the La Jolla address Rachel had given me. "He lives on a street named Fairway Road," he said. "It's probably on a golf course."

I laughed. "Wow, you could be a private eye." Would another pat on the thigh be too bold? I resisted the urge.

As Sherlock had predicted, Fairway Road was indeed on a golf course, an off-shoot of Country Club Drive. The house was a large tan Mediterranean with a red tile roof, and the entire structure was covered in some kind of ivy. Two immense palm trees stood off to the left, providing shade to most of the yard. I couldn't see through to the back, but I guessed that one of the golf course's holes was adjacent to the back yard.

We parked across the street and I dialed Block's number one last time. I wasn't exactly sure why. Courtesy?

"Someone's in there," Mike said.

"What?"

"Somebody just moved around when you called," he said.

"Was it an old man?"

"I couldn't see any details, just the shape of someone moving."

"Well, there's only one way to find out if he lives here," I said, opening the car door.

I walked up the driveway and noticed a small green Volkswagen Passat parked on a slab next to the garage. Mike waited in the car. Somebody's home, all right. I climbed up the brick steps and rang the bell. While I waited I studied the front door, which was immense and finished in a deep amber stain that brought out the richness of the mahogany. There was no answer. The window on the door was too high to peek into, and I didn't feel like snooping around, especially since Mike had seen someone inside. Someone who obviously didn't want to chat.

"So that's it?" he asked when I got back to the car.

"No, we should come back tomorrow too."

"Next time, don't call first. It only lets people know someone is looking for them."

"Good tip. For now, let's check into the hotel and get some food," I said. "I'm starving."

We arrived at our hotel in downtown San Diego around 5:30 and checked in. We met up in the lobby and the concierge pointed us in the direction of the Gas Lamp District, a historic and slightly touristy section of town about a half mile from our hotel. We stumbled upon a Mexican place with outdoor seating. I wondered briefly: do Mormons eat Mexican food? Then again, why on earth wouldn't they?

"This okay?" I asked.

"Looks good to me."

I ordered a blue margarita and Mike ordered a diet Sprite.

We studied the menus in silence. Mike decided on a baked tilapia special, while I ordered my old standby, ground beef chimichangas.

"You ever drink?" I asked.

"Once or twice. Religion says we're not supposed to, you know."

"Try mine. Just a sip." I pushed my glass in front of him. I felt like a crack dealer trying to suck in a new customer.

We locked eyes for a few seconds and he gave me a little smile. "Okay," he said, "just for you."

With his finger he wiped some of the salt off the rim of the glass. Then he took a big gulp.

"Not bad," he said. "What's all in that?"

I explained the basics of margarita mixing to him. "The key is, never order a house margarita. They sit in those giant vats all day and there's almost no booze in them."

"Good tip," he said.

The waitress returned a few minutes later with our food.

"Anything else I can get you folks?" she asked.

"I'll have a house margarita," Mike said. The waitress nodded gravely and left.

My mouth was hanging open. Mike tried to keep a straight face, but he burst out laughing.

"You bastard," I said.

"Sorry. I just had to mess with you a little. I'm not a nun, you know."

"No kidding. My great aunt's a nun and she has a pint of schnapps every day."

"I'm just like everybody else. Do you know anyone who follows every single tenet of their religion, every day, all the time?"

I thought about it for a second. "I guess not."

Mike's drink arrived, and we clinked glasses. He took a big sip out of his straw.

"Yours was better," he said.

"No shit."

About halfway through my second chimichanga I realized Mike was getting pretty drunk. I could tell because he was talking without being asked a question. He'd only finished about a quarter of his drink, but his liver was obviously out of practice.

"Drink up," I said. "They're going to think you didn't like it."

He took a big slurp. I liked men who responded to gentle nagging.

We finished up our meals and along the way he managed to drink about three-fourths of his margarita. I paid the check and slurped down the watery green dregs of his drink, which was clearly concocted with children or the elderly in mind. We left the restaurant and began walking slowly up the street.

"What now?" he asked.

I had no idea. It was only a little after seven, and I had a nice buzz going. And Mr. Titanium Thighs was feeling good. "When was the last time you had a beer?"

He giggled a little. It was an unseemly sound for a six-one guy like him, but it was kind of cute. "Is alcohol your answer for everything?"

"No. Sometimes hard drugs are required. But if you want me to drink a beer alone, I understand."

"Okay, okay. One beer. How about this place?" The bar on our right was very touristy, but it looked as good as any, and we could sit outside. Mike found a seat next to the sidewalk and I went inside to the bar.

Knowing that you're one-hundred percent definitely going to hell can be very liberating sometimes, and this was one of those times. Mike had said "one" beer, so I wanted to make it worth our while. The bartender assured me that the "imperial" amber ale they had on tap was their strongest beer, and I ordered us a couple of them in the twenty-five ounce size. The glasses were roughly a foot tall.

I hefted the two glasses onto the table like some Bavarian fraulein, somehow managing to keep most of the liquid from spilling. "What the hell is this?" Mike asked.

"I'm trying to get you drunk," I said matter-of-factly.

He shook his head in quiet resignation.

We sat for awhile in silence, watching tourists walk by in the dimming daylight. The gas street lamps fired up and came slowly to life. A cop on a chestnut horse trotted towards us. Just before passing by, the horse paused, looked directly at me, and unleashed an avalanche of poop right on the curb. God's judgment, no doubt.

I stole a furtive glance at Mike. He'd knocked off half of his beer and hadn't thrown up yet. A good sign. He was staring at the poop.

"You don't have to finish your beer just to impress me," I said. "There's a pool on the roof of our hotel, you know."

Mike looked across the table at me. His eyelids were a little droopy, but he seemed okay. He took a long look at his half a beer and gave it thoughtful consideration. "I could go for a swim," he said.

We stood up from the table. He stumbled just a bit and reached out to the table for support. I took his arm and led him out to the sidewalk. We walked together, in silence, back to the hotel.

"Meet you at the elevator in five minutes," I said.

Mike nodded somberly.

I freshened up and changed into my black bikini. I found a comfy white hotel robe in the closet and went out to the elevator. I had half expected Mike to pass out face-down on his bed, but there he was. He didn't have a robe on. Just his t-shirt and black swimming trunks.

"Good planning," I said, eyeing his shorts. His ripped thighs bulged out beneath them.

"I swim at the downtown Y almost every morning. I figured you'd spring for a hotel with a pool."

On this Monday night the pool area on the roof was deserted. Dim accent lighting highlighted a narrow lap pool that lay near the roof's edge, and an elevated hot tub stood off to the side, partially obscured by a few shrubs. We stood there surveying the scene. I took off my robe and threw it on a lounge chair. Mike looked at me and gulped.

"Holy . . ."

I smiled. "Hot tub?" I asked.

He followed behind me. My thong didn't leave much to the imagination, and I hoped he was helping himself to a good look. I bent over and pressed the button to get the bubbles going before I climbed into the tub. I watched Mike take off his shirt, revealing a muscular, lean torso and rippling arms, and for that brief moment I felt a little bit of the thrill that men must get when they come to Cougar's.

We sat quietly in the Jacuzzi for a few minutes. The sound of the pump motor running and bubbles fizzing drowned out everything else. I had been leading Mike down this path all evening, so I was pleasantly surprised when he actually took the initiative and grabbed me under the water.

"What took you so long?" I whispered.

He responded by grabbing me harder and pulling me onto his lap. He proved to be a great kisser, and I managed to keep our lips locked while I undid my top. His hands did the rest. We wriggled out of our bottoms and thrashed around the hot tub. The Mike I knew was gone, a million miles away. The new Mike still didn't speak, but his movements were confident and his hands were strong. After a minute he backed himself onto one of the stairs in the tub and pulled me onto his lap, facing him. After that, I lost all track of time and movement. I moved with him, on him, lost in the wetness of his mouth and the hot steamy water we splashed in. After an eternity of motion my arms got sore from holding onto him, but I wasn't going to let go until he was done with me. I clung tighter to his chest, and as his breathing got heavier he grabbed me even closer until it hurt. With a flurry of thrusts he heaved himself into me and finished, falling forward onto me and submerging both of us in the water. We came up gasping for air, and I put my arms around him and held him. Our chests both heaved together, seeking oxygen, and we didn't move for a very long time.

Obviously, Mike needed that. So did I. People assume that strippers must have wild and fulfilling sex lives, but most men we meet are scumbags or just plain losers. And when the good ones find out what we do for a living, they tend to back away after a few dates.

Our breathing returned to normal after a few minutes. "Want to get out?" I asked. We were still standing, holding each other, the water bubbling up to our chests.

Silence.

"Mike?"

He had fallen asleep standing up. I gave his ass a meaningful grab. "Mike? Let's go to bed."

"Okay," he murmured.

I led him slowly out of the pool, and when he got out he stood there naked, dripping wet and still half aroused. He probably thought he was in a dream. I pointed to his shirt and shorts on the ground and he seemed to get the idea. I found my robe and put it on. And then I panicked.

"Mike, did you bring your room key?"

He felt in his shorts. "No."

"Well, I'm sure they'll just give us new ones at the front desk," I said. We'd look ridiculous, but I didn't care because I was drunk and in a happy afterglowy place. Mike got his clothes on and we made our way slowly to the door. It was locked.

"What the . . ?" I pulled at the doors again. "We need a key to get back in. We're stuck out here."

He seemed not to fully appreciate the situation. He was drunker than I thought.

I looked around. "Well, it's July, we're in San Diego, and there's a bunch of cabanas over there with beds in them. It could be a lot worse. Let's go get a big drink of water first."

He followed me to the drinking fountain and drank from it like a parched mule at the Rio Grande. I led him to a cabana. He was already half asleep when we got into bed. I opened my robe and pulled his head to rest on my chest, and I fell asleep dreaming of an early morning encore.

Chapter 9

"Ex-*cooz* me, ex-*cooz* me." The high-pitched voice was insistent. As I grudgingly awoke from a peaceful sleep, I realized there was something off about the voice that I couldn't place. An accent, that was it. Mexican. I opened my eyes and squinted into the light. A wide-faced, dark skinned woman was standing in front of the cabana, her arms on her hips. Her look of disapproval didn't require any translation.

I pulled my robe around myself and propped myself up in the cabana bed. "What time is it?"

"No speak English," she said. "Ex-*cooz* me," she said again, and pointed at the door. "No open."

"Okay, I get it. We were locked out. Key?" I asked. I made a lame motion with my hand trying to explain what had happened. Mike was still asleep, face down. I shook him by the shoulders and he began producing a series of grunting noises. "We have to get out of here," I said.

"Mm hmm." He rolled over and I tried to pull him up. He seemed to finally get it and slowly raised himself from the bed. I smiled apologetically at the Mexican woman. She kept frowning at us as she looked us over. And then her eyes got big. I followed her stare to Mike's swimming trunks. It looked like he was trying to hide the Washington Monument in his shorts. I thought I caught the faintest hint of a grin on the woman's face as she turned away and waved her hands in the air in mock disgust.

"Let's go," I said.

The doors were now open, and we took the elevator down to the lobby in silence. They gave us new keys without batting an eyelash, and on the way back upstairs I couldn't tell if Mike was hung over, embarrassed, or both. We agreed to meet in the lobby coffee shop in forty-five minutes.

I was halfway through my large coffee and a bagel when Mike arrived. He got himself a glass of orange juice and a cup of yogurt mixed with fruit and granola. I was about to make fun of him, but I had a flashback to his toned, athletic body. His pecs and abs made a pretty good case for avoiding alcohol and eating right. He didn't seem too talkative, and I decided it would be better to avoid the subject of last night.

"We should probably get up to La Jolla as soon as possible," I said. "It might be a long day."

He nodded.

"You know, you don't have to come with me."

"What else am I going to do? Go shopping?" He smiled at me over his yogurt. "So," he began tentatively.

Here it comes, I thought. He wants to talk about last night. I was dreading this. Guys had a way of going weird on me—either they bailed out right after sleeping with me, or they got clingy and needy.

He continued, "You have a plan other than just going up to this guy's door and ringing the doorbell?"

"Um, actually, no."

"Okay, just checking."

Whew—I had dodged an awkward conversation. It was almost ten when the valet brought the car around. I pressed the button to drop the top down and we spent the ten miles drive up to La Jolla enjoying the warm sea air in our faces. We headed up the Pacific Highway and swung west on Mission Boulevard, which crossed over the coastal side of Mission Bay. The road hugged the coastline, and soon turned into La Jolla Boulevard. From there I retraced our route from yesterday and found the streets leading into Mel's home at the La Jolla Country Club.

As we turned onto Fairway Road, I spotted a green Volkswagen pulling into Mel's driveway a block ahead of us. I hit the brakes and began inching the car closer, trying to get a glimpse of the driver without drawing too much attention to us. I stopped a half block away and saw the car's driver—it obviously wasn't

Mel—walk up the front steps. The girl looked about twenty and had her blond hair tied back in a pony tail. She wore a gray sweatshirt and dark green shorts, and she had a grocery bag under her arm. She propped the bag up on her left hip while she used a key to let herself in.

"Well, that's not him," I said. It was not among my most insightful observations.

"Maybe that's who was moving around in there yesterday. Maybe he's renting the place out or something."

"I'm not gonna call first this time," I said. "Keep your eyes open, okay?"

I left the car parked a half block back and walked up to the house. I harbored the vague hope that if I spotted the girl through the large front window she would be forced out of embarrassment to answer the door. No such luck. I rang the bell, but again there was no answer, and I didn't detect any movement inside. What the hell was going on?

I waited a full minute but decided it would be impolite, not to mention awkward, to linger on the front porch any longer. I walked back to the Audi and slumped in the driver's seat.

"Welcome to detective work," Mike said. "A lot of sitting around doing nothing."

I was beginning to feel silly for dragging Mike along with me, although after last night I didn't regret it for a second. "So what's your professional advice? Sit here and wait?"

He sighed and began fiddling with the radio. "Let's give it a few minutes."

Ten minutes turned into twenty. Mike was still messing with the radio, which was more than a little annoying. He hadn't settled on a station yet when Mel's garage opened and a huge black Lincoln began backing up slowly out of the driveway. The car turned in our direction and began barreling down Fairway Road towards us.

"Get down," Mike said.

We both slunk down in our seats. I cursed myself for leaving the top down, but I think we managed to stay out of sight.

In the rearview mirror I saw the car wind its way north on Fairway Road and veer left when that road met up with the main country club drive. I started up the Audi and did a quick U-turn, hoping I could follow the Lincoln without being too obvious about it. By the time we came upon the end of the club drive, however, I had lost sight of the car.

"You see where it went?" I asked.

"No, but this road veers pretty sharply north. If he was going some other direction, he'd probably have turned off before now."

I bore north on Torrey Pines Road, and sure enough, at the next intersection I caught a glimpse of the Lincoln, easy to pick out amid the endless parade of smaller BMWs and Porsches that darted around La Jolla's streets. I kept following, keeping about a block's distance between us, and we veered onto La

Jolla Parkway into the heart of what was now the noon rush. After crawling along for a few blocks, the Lincoln headed for the I-5 expressway, and I followed it north at a safe distance, hoping the mass of cars on the freeway would give me some cover.

"Don't worry," I said. "I won't follow it all the way to San Francisco."

I soon began wondering how long I *would* follow the car and chided myself once again for failing to come up with any semblance of a plan ahead of time. Luckily, within ten minutes the Lincoln pulled into the right lane and exited in the town of Del Mar. There were two cars between us and the Lincoln, and the Lincoln turned left at the first road. The stoplight turned red and prevented me from following immediately, but I was able to see the car take another left at the next street up. When the light changed and I caught up, it all started to make sense. The Lincoln was three cars ahead of us in line to enter the Del Mar racetrack.

"He's playing the ponies," I said.

"A lifelong casino man, right? Makes sense. Where else you gonna find any betting action around here?"

I paid the five dollar parking fee and was careful not to trail the Lincoln too obviously, although I ended up being forced to park closer than I would have liked. The blond girl soon emerged from the driver's seat, but the passenger door opened only a crack. The girl had changed her clothes and now sported a pale yellow sun dress and fashionable oversized sunglasses. She was tall and rail-thin, with no hint of any curves beneath the dress. She was an undeniable stunner—a runway model type. I could picture her in a glossy Chanel ad splayed out on the bow of a yacht in Monaco.

The woman walked around the front of the car and pulled open the passenger door, lending her arm to help the passenger inside get out. The man who emerged was short and hunched, and he relied on his cane to stand up straight. He looked to be about eighty, with a pink face topped by an unforgivable comb-over of his wispy white hair. His frail body seemed out of place in his pressed khakis and blue blazer. His clothes made him appear distinguished and pitiful at the same time, the way a senator looks after serving one term too many.

"That must be Mel Block," I said. "Rachel said he'd be about eighty."

Mel walked slowly but steadily. We followed at a safe distance. I had never been to Del Mar in person, although I once dated a man who'd lost thousands betting on its races at Caesars Palace. It wasn't enough for him to lose, though. He had to review each race and study the racing form to figure out where he'd gone wrong, and then he'd come up with a grandiose excuse for why the race's outcome was a fluke. All of which he insisted on explaining to me. Sadly, he was one of my better boyfriends.

We made our way toward the entrance. "I don't suppose you're much of a gambler," I said.

"Got nothing against it," Mike said. "The Mormons are crystal clear on drinking and things like that, but gambling isn't quite as bad. There's even a casino town on the state border whose main business comes from Mormons crossing over from Utah."

I chuckled. "Sounds like a happening place."

Del Mar was built in a kind of laid-back Mediterranean style. Many in the early-afternoon crowd were dressed like Mel and his companion—a lot of men in blazers and women in hats and sun dresses. Luckily there were also plenty of people who, like us, had dressed for comfort.

Mel and his friend went up an escalator to a reserved deck. I soon learned that "reserved" only meant shelling out an extra fifteen bucks, and that seemed a bargain once we got inside and looked around. The deck had a private bar that resembled a lounge you'd find at an old-school L.A. hotel. There were two private betting windows for people didn't want to fight the crowds downstairs, and a bunch of tables was grouped near the railing overlooking the track. Potted ferns were everywhere.

The blonde stopped at the bar while the man I assumed was Mel found a seat at a small table next to the railing. We grabbed a seat at the table behind him. The horses below were still parading about on the paddock, and it looked like the races wouldn't start for at least another fifteen minutes. No time like the present.

"Mr. Block?" I asked softly, hoping I wouldn't startle him too much.

"Who's asking?" He craned his head around to face me. He had a pack-a-day voice, low and scratchy, but it was surprisingly vibrant.

"My name's Raven McShane," I said. "I'm working with Rachel Hannity on a project and she thought we should get in touch."

He looked me over, raised an eyebrow, and said nothing. Then he chuckled softly.

"You from Vegas?"

"Yes."

"Are you the one who's been calling me from the 702 area code?"

I nodded. "Yes, I've called a few times but there was no answer."

"A few times? I think it's been twenty."

I shrugged.

"So you had to follow me to the race track?" He turned around fully to face me. "This must be some project."

"Well, it's pretty important. Rachel thought you could help me get a handle on some things and . . ." I stopped in mid-sentence. "So how come you didn't answer your phone?" I was more than a little curious. And ticked.

He shook his head back and forth, his face more serious. "It's kind of personal. If you really want to know, I owe a lot of people money back there, and they only managed to track me down here a few months ago. Since then there have been any number of bill collectors and lawyers calling me, and I've been playing hard to get, you might say. Sorry for the inconvenience." He looked at Mike for the first time. "Your friend?"

Mike introduced himself.

Just then the young woman returned with a glass of white wine for herself and what looked like a martini on the rocks for Mel. He flashed us a mischievous look that suggested we would be better off if we didn't make any editorial comments about his supermodel companion or his pre-noon cocktail. He attempted to introduce us to his young friend.

"Nicole, this is . . ." he stopped, obviously forgetting our names.

Mike shot out of his seat like a Marine corporal coming to attention for a four-star general. "Mike Caffrey," he said, taking her hand. "Nice to meet you. This is Raven McShane."

Nicole's greeting was pleasant but wary. She'd probably learned to be cagey at the Chanel modeling school. But she smiled faintly at Mike, and I immediately began to like her a lot less.

"Sorry," Mel said, "I'm getting old. Nicole is my in-home assistant and caregiver. Honey," he smiled indulgently, "these folks have some business to talk over with me. Would you mind taking a look at the horses in the first race?"

"Of course," she said, knowing she was being dismissed.

"She's actually got a great eye for winners," Mel said. All three of us admired Nicole as she walked away. I wondered if it hurt to sit down when your ass was that small.

"I don't want to take up too much of your time on a nice day like this," I started. The old man's eyes glistened with interest, but he kept quiet. "Anyway, I managed to get myself banned from the casino, so you're the only person I have left to talk to."

"*Banned*?" he squawked incredulously. "Who banned you?"

"A guy named Holman and another guy with a mustache. He didn't say much."

"Hmm," he grunted. "Holman's head of security, works for Phil d'Angelo."

I nodded.

"He's also a schmuck," Mel mumbled.

"Among other things."

Mel shrugged. "And what makes you think I would just start singing like a canary? Or that I even have any dirt to dish?" His gaze was directed down at the track, where Nicole had begun dutifully inspecting the horses as they pranced by. Mike was watching her too, I noticed. I elbowed him sharply in the ribs. "She's too young for you," I hissed under my breath.

Mike put up his hands in a protest of innocence. Mel seemed amused by the whole thing.

I turned back to Mel. "I don't know if you know anything," I said. "But we did drive all the way down here just to talk to you." He turned to face me, and I leaned towards him to give a better view of my cleavage. Shameless, but effective. Nicole might have a great pair of legs, but she didn't have a rack built by the finest plastic surgeon in L.A. "What I'm really interested in is anything you might know about the murder of George Hannity."

He looked up from my chest. "Jesus, you don't mess around."

I smiled back at him.

"Look, I heard the same rumors other people heard, and I'm certainly not buddy-buddy with the crowd running the place now. Did you know they got rid of me?" He pulled a short cigar out of his coat pocket. "I'd offer you one, but I wasn't expecting cigar-smoking company today."

"No problem," I said. "I like them much bigger than that, anyway. So why did they get rid of you?"

He seemed amused by the question. "No hard feelings on my part, actually. That was three years ago and they were the new guard. I should have retired long ago anyway. But those are people you don't want to be messing with, let me just put it that way. They have a good thing going, and they're not going to take kindly to some stranger poking around." He took a big loud slurp of his martini and then lit his cigar with a match. "Even if that stranger is a stunning beauty like yourself," he added. There was a friendly yet devilish twinkle in his eyes.

I pretended to ignore the compliment, but I made sure to store it in my compliment bank for future reference and re-examination. "So you didn't hear any gossip one way or the other whether Cody actually killed George?"

"Nope. After Cody got off, I don't think anyone who actually knew anything was in the mood to stir up that pot."

"Including you?" I asked.

He chuckled, letting loose a big puff of cigar smoke. He pointed his cigar at Mike. "Does this guy talk, or do I have to pull a string?"

"I'm her boss," Mike deadpanned. "Just here to make sure she doesn't screw things up."

Mel shrugged. "I wouldn't know anything about the murder," he said, "but—".

I raised my eyebrows expectantly.

"I shouldn't really be telling you this," he said, sighing. He slumped a bit in his chair, and he turned to look down on Nicole and the sun-drenched racetrack below. "I'm dying," he said simply, catching me completely off-guard. "I don't know exactly when, but this is probably my last summer."

I wasn't good at sympathetic utterances, so I just sat there in silence. Several seconds passed before he spoke again.

"Anyway, I didn't know exactly what was going on," he explained, "but I had a hunch before I left that some people were taking some liberties with the books. Not nickel-and-dime stuff either. By the time I left I was pretty sure that the casino was making more money than it was reporting to the owners."

"Or the IRS," Mike said.

"So they were stealing?" I asked. "Why didn't you tell anyone this before?" I asked.

He thought for a moment, holding his cigar up to his face to inspect the evenness of the burn. "That's a fair question. For one, I didn't have much proof. I just noticed people were living a little higher on the hog than their salaries justified. A lot of closed-door meetings. And two, I'm just plain greedy. Do you know that even though they basically threw me out on my ass, they pay me twenty-thousand dollars a month in a pension? Out of the blue. I didn't have any pension coming to me at all. I thought it was a mistake at first, but when I asked about it they told me to enjoy retirement and remember my friends at the casino."

"So you think it's hush money?" I asked.

"Basically. I know where a lot of bodies are buried, and I put in twenty-six years in that place. They weren't going to take any chances on my loyalty, let's put it that way. I had a few million saved up already, but with the pension I began developing some expensive habits," he said, gesturing at the racetrack below. I couldn't tell whether he meant the horses or Nicole.

"Who did you talk to about the pension?" I asked.

"Whom."

"Sorry?"

"Never mind," he said. "Phil d'Angelo—he's in charge of all the numbers, the books, that sort of thing."

Nicole waved at us from the track below.

Mel smiled indulgently. He felt the need to unburden himself. "Since my wife passed four years ago, Nicole's been the highlight of my life. For eight hundred a week, she cooks, cleans and takes me places three days a week. There's no simpler pleasure I know these days than to park myself in a chair in the backyard and watch her mow the lawn. Nothing but a red bikini top and jean shorts. Back and forth she goes, back and forth." He chuckled. "She's usually lost in whatever music she's got on her headphones. But she knows I'm watching and I think she secretly kind of likes the attention." He looked at Mike conspiratorially. "Those legs of hers," he said wistfully. "They're about all that's getting me out of bed these days."

Mike nodded gravely, and I let the horny old man think about Nicole's legs for a few more seconds. "About the management," I said, "do you think Cody was involved in cooking the books?"

"Could be," he said, taking another long puff of his cigar. "Honestly, I didn't know him that well. When he came in to work there it was more as a hobby, I think. You know, he was basically a trophy house husband whose wife owned part of the place. He was just a stage dancer, you know, and I think he wanted to look and act like he was a businessman or something. Phil D'Angelo really runs things over there."

"I can relate to that," I blurted out. Cody and I had something in common: we both wanted to find something more productive to do than taking our clothes off for money.

Mel drained the rest of his martini as if it were his last, and he turned to face me directly. "It wouldn't surprise me if my hunch about embezzlement was part of the reason George Hannity was killed, if that's what you're getting at. He was a tough owner and a straight shooter. Not everyone was thrilled to have him lurking around."

"And if he found out anyone was ripping him off, the gravy train would end?"

"Could be. Wouldn't be the first time someone was murdered in that town to protect the skim." He chuckled knowingly.

"That stuff was before my time," I said. "Or I thought it was, anyway."

"In the good old days," Mel said, "the casinos were run by the mob and financed by union pension funds. Anyone who threatened the skim would be shot, execution style. Don't think everyone's a boy scout all of a sudden."

He didn't need to tell me that. After all, I'd been backroomed like a common card counter just last week. "You've been very helpful." I elbowed Mike and stood up. "Thank you for talking with us."

"Did I have a choice?" he asked, grinning broadly and grabbing my arm with a little affection. "Sorry you had to come all the way out here to find me," he added. "But I'm *very* glad I got to see you in person."

"And if anyone asks," I said reassuringly, "I didn't hear anything about the casino from you."

He winked. "At this point, you can give them all the finger for me." Nicole returned with another martini for Mel, although this one clearly had more ice than gin in it. Smart woman. I handed Mel a business card in case he thought of anything else later, and we left the two of them to enjoy the races in peace.

Chapter 10

Mike and I took the escalator down to join the rest of the unwashed masses in the cheap seats. "Nicole seemed to like you," I said.

"Why do you say that?"

"She didn't twist her face into a disgusted frown when she looked at you."

"Oh."

"I was beginning to get jealous."

Mike grunted. Apparently the topic of conversation didn't interest him.

He looked thoughtful on our walk back to the car. "So what do you think?"

"You mean, is that enough to nail Cody Masterson?"

He nodded. "If Mel's hunch is right, Cody's got a steady flow of tax-free cash coming in. That's hard to give up."

"Tax free and partner-free, too," I added. "If Cody's been skimming money off the top, he would have been stealing from George. If George had found out he was getting ripped off . . ." I trailed off.

Mike finished my thought. "I can't think of a better reason for Cody to blow George's brains out on a deserted highway. Especially if George was about to end it or turn Cody in to the cops."

We left the racetrack parking lot and made our way back downtown to the hotel, where we checked out. Mike was quiet for most of the drive back to Vegas. I wasn't sure if he was lost in thought or just hung over. He hadn't said a peep about last night, and I was beginning to wonder if he even remembered our romp in the hot tub. We hit the Nevada border around four o'clock, and that seemed to rouse Mike out of his thoughts.

"This Mel guy didn't seem too sure that Cody was actually involved in this skim business," he said.

"Is that what you've been thinking about all this time?"

"No. I have a headache, that's all. How much did I have to drink last night?"

"Not too much. A gringo margarita and a half a beer." I didn't mention that the half beer was probably as strong as two normal beers.

"Huh. Anyway, your problem is still the same," he said. "Something like a skim is hard to prove. It's a complicated process that's all done on the inside, and you happen to have gotten yourself banned from the place."

"Are you volunteering to help me?"

"No. I do actually have some of my own cases, you know."

"But they're not as much fun as working with me, are they?"

"True." He smiled. "But let's face it. I've lived in Vegas for fifteen years. I remember the FBI once spent two years proving a single case of skimming. They had informants on the inside, specially trained agents, accountants, handwriting experts, marked bills, wiretaps, and God knows what else. And you're just you."

"Thanks for the vote of confidence."

"My point is, I don't think you want to open that whole can of worms. And you don't have to. The details of the skim aren't that important right now, or at least that's not what your client hired you to sniff out. That would take forever, and for you it'd be impossible. The real question is, did George Hannity find out about a skim before he was killed? And if so, was Cody involved?"

"I don't think I'm with you all the way," I said.

"The point is that any embezzlement operation is irrelevant unless you can show that George Hannity had actually found out about it. Otherwise there'd be no reason to kill him. So if you can show that he knew about it, and if you can show that Cody's tied into the whole thing, that might be enough to take him down."

I nodded. "I get it. If I find out Hannity knew nothing about it, I can drop it and focus on other things. No sense going off on a wild goose chase if I don't have to."

"Exactly." Mike had a good point.

We got back to Las Vegas just in time for the tail end of rush hour, and I dropped Mike off his house. He gave me a smile and thanked me for dragging him along. But that was it. Shy Mike was back.

I got home and checked my mail. I was surprised to find a cashier's check for $4,500 along with a copy of my retainer agreement signed by Barbara Finley, the woman from Indiana who'd called the week before. I was almost certain she'd been scared off by my hourly rates, but I was happy to be wrong. As instructed, Barbara included a note describing what she'd sniffed out about her husband's itinerary. He'd be arriving Thursday morning on Northwest Airlines flight 903, staying at Mandalay Bay with a party of five or six, leaving Sunday. She'd also enclosed a few pictures of her husband to help me identify him. Easy work—no hassle, paid up front, nobody gets hurt. The best part was that clients like Mrs. Finley were always happiest when I had nothing interesting to report.

The sun was creeping lower and lower, and after the long road trip all I wanted to do was open a bottle of champagne and lounge on my balcony to watch the

Strip light up at night. Actually, what I really wanted was for Mike to join me in the hot tub in the pool downstairs, but it seemed like he only put out after tequila. I made a solemn resolution to get him drunk more often.

In a rare moment of genius I came up with a way to be lazy and get some work done at the same time. I could call Rachel. We hadn't talked much about my progress so far. Probably because I hadn't *made* any progress. I picked up the phone and dialed her cell number.

"How'd you like to come over for some champagne? We can order food and watch the Strip light up from my balcony."

"Um, okay. What's the occasion?"

"Just want to talk a little about the case." I cringed, unable to believe my own fib. I fessed up. "Actually, it's really just an excuse to open some bubbly."

She laughed. "You need an excuse? Just give me your address and I'll get there in a half hour."

That gave me enough time to dig out a few bottles I had stashed away underneath my bed. One for the freezer, one for the fridge. I was glad Rachel was joining me. We'd been great friends five years ago, but things had changed when she married George. But even after George was killed Rachel didn't make any efforts to restart our friendship. I supposed that once you were admitted to high society, there wasn't much reason to rekindle old friendships with commoner like me.

Rachel was on time. It was still over 90 degrees outside, and she was dressed for it. She wore casual athletic shorts, sandals, and a thin brown zip-up cotton top. When we got outside to my balcony, she removed the top. She knew I was checking her out, so she made a little display out of it by swinging her top around above her head. She was pushing forty, but she looked fantastic in the skimpy red bra she wore underneath. The washed-out Rachel I'd seen at Cougar's a week earlier was gone.

"You look great," I said. "Every time I see you, I think I should have gone with C's. Mine are too big."

"That's crap and you know it," she said, smiling. "By the way, your valet guy is *gorgeous*! He can park my car anytime."

"Must be Tommy. Working late."

She smiled lasciviously. "Yum! Now where's this champagne you promised?"

I got out a couple glasses and poured from the bottle that had been in the freezer. It wasn't quite cold enough yet, but we didn't care. We clinked glasses, took healthy gulps, and settled into the two reclining deck chairs on my balcony. The giant fake hot air balloon outside the Paris casino was beginning to glow a deep blue.

"I was in San Diego the last two days," I said. "Finally found Mel Block."

"So he's still alive?"

"Yeah, but not for long. He's got a nice pad in La Jolla and a little waif who acts as his maid. Anyway, he has a theory that some insiders might have been skimming profits from the casino."

"When?"

"He thought it's been going on for awhile, but he was short on details. More of a hunch kind of thing. He just knows they've been paying him an awful lot of money for no apparent reason. He thinks it's so he keeps his mouth shut."

"Wow," she muttered.

"So George never mentioned anything about this? He wasn't suspicious that someone was ripping him off from the inside?"

Rachel thought about it for a second. "Not that I remember. He would have gone through the roof, though. As hard as he worked for that place—and his dad, too—to think that someone would be stealing from him is pretty scary. Especially if it was his brother-in-law."

"No doubt." We'd managed to polish off our champagne in less than five minutes. I poured us fresh glasses.

"So does Mel think Cody was involved in this?"

"He wasn't sure, but he thought it was possible. So you're sure George never mentioned anything about this?"

"Yeah, I'm sure. I would remember something like that. If they were stealing from George, they were stealing from me!"

"Good point," I said.

"I suppose you might try talking to Amy herself. I never really talked about business with George, but he and his sister were pretty tight. She might have known if something was up."

I refilled my glass again. "That will be a fun conversation. Hi, I'm wondering if your husband was stealing from the casino and murdered your brother when he found out. Can we talk?"

"Yeah, I guess I hadn't thought about it that way," Rachel said.

"Anyway, it's too nice a night to talk about business. But I think now I can officially deduct the champagne as a business expense."

"Happy to help," she said. "Can you deduct Chinese food too?" Her eyelids were getting a little droopy. I had forgotten what a lightweight she was.

"I don't see why not." I went inside to get a menu, and we decided on the Happy Family Special, which seemed to come with two helpings of every kind of fried meat I could imagine.

It was still hot outside, and we sat like steamed dumplings as we waited for our food and watched the daylight fade to black. Rachel was well past her limit for champagne.

She turned to look at me suddenly. "You getting any these days?"

"Any what?" I asked.

She smiled mischievously.

"What are you, in high school?" I laughed.

She frowned. "I take that as a 'no.'"

"Actually, I should thank you. My little San Diego trip gave me an excuse to get out of town with this guy I kind of work with."

"Do tell." She turned her recliner a few degrees to face me.

"Well, he's kind of shy. Mike's his name. Actually, he's supposed to be supervising my work during my first year as an investigator."

"So . . . he's ugly?"

I chuckled. "Not even close. You should see his abs. Anyway, he's a Mormon, and like I said, he's kind of shy."

"So the answer is, 'no, you're not getting any.'" Rachel made a face.

"Not exactly. After a couple of drinks, Mike turned into a beast."

"I thought Mormons don't drink," she said.

"Just like Catholics never miss church on Sundays."

"So you got him drunk?" She pretended to be shocked.

"It was worth it," I said. "And the guy's like thirty-five. He's a big boy. A very big boy, actually." An X-rated image of a dripping wet naked Mike popped into my head.

She raised her eyebrows. "So are you guys an item?"

"An item? Who says that anymore?" I chuckled. "No, I doubt it. He didn't even kiss me goodbye when I dropped him off at home."

"Wow," she said. We sat in silence for a minute. "So how drunk did you get this poor young man?"

I thought about it for a second. "He was pretty tanked, I guess. Why?"

"Well, are you sure he remembers sleeping with you? That happened to me once when I was in college. Guy got me drunk and apparently we had a lot of fun that I will never remember. He was offended when I barely said 'hi' to him the next day."

"That only happened *once*?"

She shot me a dirty look.

"I suppose it's possible," I said. "Mike never mentioned it today and he acted almost like nothing had happened." That would explain a lot, I thought. I poured off the rest of the bottle right before our Happy Family special arrived. It made us very happy indeed, but we both developed a food coma and passed out watching a Lifetime movie.

Chapter 11

The morning news said we had finally been granted a reprieve from the weather, with high temperatures only expected to reach the low 90's. The downside was that I had no more excuses for avoiding my daily jog. I toughed it up and got my jogging clothes on. I ran west from my apartment, away from the Strip into a maze of strip malls, warehouses and the occasional pawn shop. The first half of the jog was a blissful escape. I thought about everything and nothing at the same time. But reality hit me when I turned to head back. I was nowhere in this case. I had learned almost nothing about the Outpost casino except that its head of security was an asshole with sharp fingernails. The only lead I had was what Mel Block had told me at the Del Mar racetrack, but how was I supposed to learn anything about a skim operation if I couldn't even get inside the place?

Rachel said it might be worth talking with Amy Masterson, her former sister-in-law. I had poured cold water on that idea. It didn't take a genius to guess that Amy wouldn't be in any kind of a mood to help anyone trying to prove her husband was a murderer. And I would be willing to bet that word had already gotten out that I had been sniffing around about Cody Masterson.

As I cooled down from my jog, a growing temptation was building in me to pawn the problem off on Mike. He had tried to look busy earlier in the week, but I could tell he wasn't exactly swamped in his own work. It was the dead of summer, and a lot of the insurance people he worked for were probably on vacation. Plus, it might give me an opportunity to get him drunk again.

I showered quickly and hit the internet. I had no idea where a jet-set couple like Amy and Cody Masterson might live—a palatial suburban mansion? Lake Las Vegas? A penthouse condo on the Strip? I guessed that they were not listed in the phonebook, and I was right. The two were hardly a publicity-shy couple, though, so I figured their home would have been in the newspaper at some point.

I searched the *Review-Journal*'s website for any stories mentioning their house. Nada. The Mastersons hadn't hosted any charity galas or political fundraisers, apparently. I decided I might as well pay for the information. Rachel hadn't said anything about money, and I hadn't felt like bringing it up. But I assumed if things worked out she'd pay me a small fortune without me having to ask. I had a Westlaw account, and with that online service you could uncover all sorts of legal information about real estate—deeds, easements, title transfers, or even overdue property taxes. Plugging in a search for AMY MASTERSON didn't produce any hits, but when I used her maiden name, AMY HANNITY, I found three records. The first hit showed that she had purchased a $755,000 house in the east side of town about eight years ago. The second record, five years later, told me she sold that house for a nifty $400,000 profit, and the third hit revealed that she'd plowed that money into a property assessed at $2.6 million on Champion Hills Lane in the western suburb of Spring Valley, about ten miles away from the Strip. I wondered how much the street's pretentious name added to the purchase price.

I wrote down the address and phoned Mike. He didn't sound too thrilled with the idea.

"If anything, *you're* supposed to be working for *me*," he said. I wondered if he was a little sensitive about the whole thing. He was the one with the experience, but I was the one working the big case while he chased down small-time deadbeats who were faking neck injuries. I decided to become a damsel in distress.

"I just don't know where else to turn," I said. "I'm toxic. They won't let me in that casino, and everyone connected with it probably knows I'm trying to bring Cody down."

Mike gave me his silent routine.

"I've already done the hard part," I said.

"Meaning what?"

"I found out where she lives."

He snorted. "What exactly am I supposed to do? Ring the doorbell and ask, 'Did your husband do it?'"

I explained what I wanted to know, which was whether she or her brother had any idea that someone inside the casino was ripping them off.

"I guess that makes sense," he said. "If I come in asking whether her brother knew they were being stolen from, it's not quite as bad as asking if her husband's a murderer."

"Right. All I want to know is if George suspected any kind of embezzlement before he was killed. She might actually be interested in finding out someone thinks they're being ripped off. If Cody was involved, it's very possible that she has no idea about it."

"And I can bill this?" Mike asked.

"Of course!" I laughed. That didn't mean he'd be *paid* for it, but I didn't mention that little detail. "I figure she might be home right now actually. It's only ten. How about it?"

"You're driving?"

"Whatever it takes. I'll just hide in the car when we get there."

I called down to the valet to get my car. When I got downstairs, Tommy was bent over my car polishing the hood. No one seemed to be watching, so I allowed myself ten seconds to admire the view. At what point, I wondered, did I officially become a dirty old woman?

I headed downtown to pick up Mike at his office, and then we headed west on Vegas Drive, which formed a T with a street called Rampart Boulevard.

"Nice neighborhood," Mike said. "They don't mess around out here."

Rampart Boulevard lived up to its name. An imposing twelve-foot stone wall ran the entire length of the street, basically giving the finger to the outside world and anyone who didn't belong there.

"Nothing subtle about that wall," I said. "Gotta keep the riffraff away."

Mike chuckled. "Riffraff like us."

I had worked at a few private events in homes in this neighborhood—birthday and bachelor parties, mostly—but I wasn't about to let Mike know that. I drove south along the wall for a few blocks and found the entrance to the subdivision. Summerlin, as the entire community was known, was an upscale development consisting mainly of condos and mansions, and several of the neighborhoods were gated. For some reason, this wasn't one of them.

We wound our way around streets with annoying names like Trophy Hills Drive and found the Mastersons' house at one end of Champion Hills Lane. Another golf course estate. Mel Block's pad in La Jolla looked downright modest by comparison.

"That's the TPC behind the house," Mike said.

I gave him a blank stare.

"Tournament Players Club. They have a PGA event there every year."

"Of course. You a golfer?"

He nodded.

I sighed. "Well, nobody's perfect."

The Mastersons' home was not the typical Mediterranean-style villa that seemed so omnipresent in the southwest. Instead, it was a French-inspired chateau, all stone, complete with a three-story half-turret.

"Looks like the architect took the design right off the label of a bottle of French wine," I said.

Mike smiled. "A French chateau next to a golf course, in the middle of the desert."

I chuckled. "Ten miles away from a fake Eiffel Tower, a giant pyramid, and a volcano that explodes every fifteen minutes."

"Don't forget the pirate show," he said.

I parked a few houses up the street, and Mike got out. He was wearing his bible salesman outfit again: short-sleeved white shirt, red tie, gray slacks, black shoes. I moved over to the passenger seat and watched him approach the door. He paused a second before ringing the bell, and in that instant a blonde woman in running clothes emerged.

Amy Masterson looked startled. She was obviously on her way out for a run and wasn't expecting to find someone lingering at her front door. She took the headphones out of her ears, and the two of them talked. After a few minutes she unfolded her arms and seemed to relax a bit. She and Mike went inside.

Mike was in the house for what seemed like an eternity. After a half-hour, I considered sneaking up to the house myself to see what was going on. My womanly sense was beginning to prickle, but I laughed it off. Mike was as smooth as sandpaper, and Amy was married—to Cody Masterson, no less, reputedly the sexiest man in Las Vegas. I convinced myself I had no reason to suspect any hanky panky.

The front door finally opened and Amy showed Mike out. I slunk down in my seat in case she looked in my direction. Mike looked a little unsettled when he got back to the car.

Mike backed the car up a hundred feet or so and then did a U-turn to get out of the subdivision. I was still crouched down in my seat.

"How'd it go?" I asked.

"Well, I don't know if she bought it or not. But she didn't exactly throw me out of her house, either."

"Did she have anything useful to say?"

"Not really. She said she didn't notice any change in George before he was killed. She and her brother talked business almost every day, and she doubted there was any funny business going on with their books. George probably would have known about it, she said."

"That's the question, though. Did he find out about it right before being killed? Or was he *about* to discover it?"

"Amy didn't think so. But like you said, who knows whether George might have been hot on the trail. George could have started nosing around, and Cody got nervous and decided to kill him before he figured out what was going on."

"Well it looks like another dead end," I said. "Cody wasn't at home, was he?"

"No sign of him. Actually, when I was there she got a phone call from another man, and they sounded pretty, uh, friendly."

"How so?" I asked.

"It sounded like they were making weekend plans. I thought that was kind of strange."

"And it wasn't Cody?"

"No, she called him something else. Eddie."

"Huh." In the last week I had looked at about two dozen pictures of Cody in the newspaper. If I had a man who looked like him, I wouldn't be spending weekends canoodling with someone else.

We hit a long stoplight heading back downtown. "So what were you guys doing in there for so long?" I tried not to sound accusatory, but I was dying to find out.

He started blushing. "She's a very friendly woman, let's just say that."

"What happened in there, Casanova?"

He laughed. "Nothing happened. She just, well, she wanted to show me her bedroom and . . ."

The light turned green and my foot overreacted on the gas pedal. Mike's head was thrown back into the headrest.

"Ouch," he said.

He deserved it. "So you went up to her bedroom, and . . ."

"She said it was just remodeled."

"I suppose she wanted to show you her needlework too?"

"No. Eventually she got on the bed and suggested I join her there."

"And?"

"And that's when I left."

"Wow." That little hussy. I took a deep breath. "Sorry, I didn't mean to cross-examine you. You're a grown-up. You can do whatever you want."

Mike just looked at me and smiled. I had a hard time picturing him getting angry or losing his cool.

"Oh, I did learn one other little tidbit," Mike said. His eyes were sparkling with amusement. "I called her 'Mrs. Masterson' and she busted a gut. She said Cody's name is bogus. His parents emigrated from Sweden to Minnesota, so he's first generation. His real name is Lars Bergstrom."

I laughed out loud. "Well, it's no wonder he changed it. Not exactly a showbiz name." *Lars*, I thought. That was precious. "But here's what I don't get. Amy's husband—Cody, Lars, whatever his name is—is supposed to be the best looking guy in Vegas. Why would she have a guy on the side *and* then try to put the moves on you, too?"

"Maybe Cody's got someone on the side himself," he said. "But why are you so surprised? I *am* pretty irresistible."

I decided to play along. "Oh, I don't blame her at all for throwing herself at you. Especially with that sexy shirt and tie combo you're wearing today. That Ward Cleaver look is really making a comeback."

He sighed.

"So are you sure it was some kind of boyfriend she was talking to on the phone?

"Pretty sure," he said.

"When were they leaving for this weekend getaway?"

"It sounded like tomorrow. Thursday through Sunday."

"You're quite the little spy," I said admiringly.

We pulled up to Mike's office building around noon. I fluttered my eyelashes and smiled at him.

"Now what?" he asked.

"I've got another client, a guy coming in from Indiana that I'm supposed to keep an eye on."

"I do have other work, you know," Mike said. "You can't handle two things at once?"

"I can, but I'm not a very good tail. For some reason I find it impossible to fade into the background. One guy a few months ago asked me if I was stalking him. And that was after only twenty minutes."

"Can't you, you know, cover yourself up a little? Try to look a little less . . . noticeable?"

I laughed. "Is that a compliment?"

"You're a very pretty young woman," he said.

What was I, his niece? "Thank you," I said. "I suppose I could try wearing a sweatshirt and maybe a baseball cap. But only if I can't find someone else to do it."

"Sorry, Raven. Looks like you're doing your own dirty work on this one."

I sighed. "Thanks for coming with today, though."

"Two and a quarter hours," he said.

"I'll make a note of it."

I headed home and called Carlos Villaregosa, my bouncer friend from Cougar's. The husband of Barbara Finley, the nervous housewife from Indiana, was arriving the next morning, and I was planning to sleep in. Carlos had tagged along with me a few times before, and he'd never turned down an easy paycheck. He didn't disappoint. I gave Carlos the details of Finley's arrangements and scanned one of his photos and emailed it to him. Following this guy around was something Carlos could do by himself.

"A bachelor party. Nice," he said. "Maybe they'll end up at Cougar's."

"Yeah, then you can work both jobs at the same time."

"It's called efficiency."

"You have a camera?" I asked.

"Cell phone."

"Good enough, I guess. Just let me know if he gets himself in trouble."

Chapter 12

I danced at Cougar's until the wee hours on Wednesday night and slept in on Thursday. I decided to take most of the day off. It wasn't a difficult decision: I had zilch to go on and my phone hadn't exactly been ringing off the hook with other work. And what had seemed like a nugget of useful information from Mel Block hadn't produced any significant new leads to go on. Neither Rachel nor Amy had noticed anything unusual about George's behavior before he was killed, and no one besides Mel seemed to think that anyone was ripping the place off. If George hadn't found out about any kind of skim operation, there wasn't much point in poking that hornet's nest.

After lunch I went shopping at the Palazzo. I was drooling over a pair of Christian Louboutin leopard print pumps when one of the waifish clerks shot a death stare at me. It wasn't completely her fault. She was new, and I was dressed like a mid-priced whore who had no business looking at a seven-hundred-dollar pair of shoes. But still, I didn't like her. In fact, as a general rule I hated anyone that thin.

I waved at her and she reluctantly came over. Her nametag said her name was Marissa. "Do you have these in a size nine?" I asked.

She made a face. "I'll have to check in back." Oh, the horror.

She returned and shoved a shoebox at me. I sat down and tried them on. They looked fantastic on me. Not that Marissa would admit it. She was a big time clerk at a shoe store, after all.

"I'll take them," I said.

Her mask of superiority vanished for a split second, and she flashed me the briefest of smiles. A real human being was in there, somewhere. Unfortunately for her I had already decided I was going to out-bitch her.

"Just have Claire put it on my tab," I said, handing her my driver's license. Claire was the manager. She had sold me two dozen pairs since the store opened two years ago, and I had an open line of credit. That meant Claire would get the commission and not the witchy Marissa. I felt a pang of remorse, but it passed quickly.

I browsed around some of the other stores, but it turned out I wasn't in a shopping mood. Something was nagging at me about Mike's experience with Amy Masterson, and it wasn't just misplaced jealousy. Not too long ago, Amy's husband Cody had made women scream and throw their panties on stage when he danced. It bugged me that his wife would now be so starved for male attention that she apparently had a guy on the side and was hot to get Mike into bed as well. It didn't make sense. It was starting to look like there might be more to Cody's and Amy's marriage than met the eye. I found a bench in the mall and called Rachel.

I caught her in her car. "Quick question," I said. "How are Cody and Amy as a couple? Are they close?"

"I think so," she said. "At least I've never heard otherwise. Why?"

I told her about Mike's encounter with Amy.

"Huh. I guess I haven't really socialized with them much since George died. They could be fighting or something for all I know."

"Ok, thanks."

I didn't have anything else to go on, so I figured it might be an angle worth exploring. Amy had been Cody's only alibi witness during the trial, corroborating his story that they'd both been at home together in bed on the night of the murder. Bad habits don't come out of the blue. If they were cheating on each other now, I figured there was a chance they were cheating back then. It wasn't much, but it was something. If I could show that they weren't really happily married at the time George Hannity was murdered, it would undercut their story that they were together in bed when the murder happened.

From the scraps Mike had overheard of Amy's telephone conversation, it sounded like she was being picked up at home by "Eddie" later that night. Mike had no idea what time.

Carlos called my cell while I was walking back from the Palazzo. He reported that the bachelor party group had checked into the Mandalay Bay hotel, and for the time being they were sunning themselves at the pool. Carlos was bored.

"You up for a change of pace?" I asked.

"I'm gonna fall asleep watching these guys," he said. "I got class at seven, though."

"Class?"

"I'm in summer school."

"Getting your G.E.D.?"

He was silent for several seconds. "No. I'm six credits short of my MBA."

Oops. Carlos and I were casual work friends, but by design I hadn't gotten too personal with him. "Wow, you're a regular Alex P. Keaton."

"Who?"

I guessed that Carlos was only five or six years younger than I was, but these days that felt like an entire generation. "Never mind. Anyway, I'm going to sit outside a house in Summerlin, try to get a few photos."

"Somehow I thought your life would be a little more exciting."

"Come on, it'll be fun."

"Why you need me?"

I figured he was trying to work me for more money. I decided to call his bluff. "Yeah, you're right. You should focus on your studies. Forget it."

"Okay, fine. It's just a marketing class," he said. "I can skip it."

I said I'd pick him up outside of Mandalay Bay around 5:30 and we'd head over to Summerlin. I hopped in the shower when I got home. When I dried off my phone was beeping at me. Change of plans. Carlos had left a message saying the bachelor party was headed over to the Red Rock Casino, and he wanted to know if he should follow them or come with me. I called him back and told him to follow them there. Red Rock was only a few miles from the Masterson house, and I said I would swing by and pick him up there around 6:15.

I reached the casino around six and used the self-park. The Red Rock was a trendy off-Strip resort geared toward people who wanted luxury in the desert but didn't want to fight the crowds on the Strip. From what Carlos had said, the Indiana bachelor party was just looking for a change of scenery to play some craps. Nothing too risqué for a Thursday afternoon. Red Rock had five craps tables in action, and I spotted Carlos pretending to play a slot machine near one of them. He was wearing a black White Sox cap tilted sideways and baggy black jeans. An oversized baby blue UCLA basketball jersey hung loosely over a tight white t-shirt.

"Any luck?" I asked, nodding at the slot machine.

Carlos pretended to look disgusted and started shaking his head at me in disapproval. "G.E.D. my ass," he muttered. "I was top twenty percent in business at UNLV."

"Thanks for the résumé update." I wondered briefly why he spent his nights working at a strip club instead of some corporate gig or something. Oh wait, I think I know.

"Anyway, no, I haven't won anything from this stupid machine. I put a quarter in but I still haven't pressed 'spin,'" he said. "The math is against you, so why play?"

"Shhhh," I hissed. "Saying things like that could get you killed in this town."

He smiled. "I'm not afraid."

I glanced over at the group of men standing at the craps table. "How are your boys doing?"

"How are your girls doing?" He made a show of looking down my shirt.

I sighed. "You've seen me buck naked a thousand times. Can't you keep your head at eye level for two minutes?"

He shrugged. "I know what I like," he said.

"You better behave yourself, or I'll tell your girlfriend."

He looked genuinely scared. "Okay, okay." He tilted his head toward the craps table. "That fat guy is Finley."

"Fat guy" was being kind. Richard Finley's three hundred pounds didn't sit very comfortably on his five-seven frame.

"Seems kind of like a square," I said.

Carlos nodded. "More like a blob. But you're right. When they got here, the whole group bought cigars. A few of them giggled like little girls when they lit up."

"Yikes. They probably think drinking caffeinated coffee is wild and crazy. So Finley is the best man. Which one's the groom?"

"I think it's that guy with the sunglasses."

"Looks like another winner," I said. "He thinks he's Roy Orbison?"

"Who?"

I sighed. "He's the guy who invented wearing sunglasses indoors. Ever hear the song *Pretty Woman*?"

Carlos gave me a blank look, and I decided it was hopeless. We both turned discreetly to watch the group play craps.

The woman shooting the dice was a gray-haired librarian type who looked befuddled by the whole game. She was probably just being a good sport by rolling the dice for her husband's sake, I figured. The woman managed only four rolls of the dice before crapping out. The whole table groaned in unison, but

Finley and his nerdy bachelor party didn't seem too upset by their bad luck.

"You got some pics of them?"

Carlos scrolled through a few photos he'd taken on his cell phone. "Why do you need pictures?"

"I don't, but I like to show the client I actually did my job. They tend to get suspicious if I just tell them I didn't see anything and then cash their check for five grand. Anyway, these guys don't seem like they're going to get into much trouble today. Let's get out of here."

Chapter 13

Although it had cooled off a little this week, the parking garage was still brutally hot when we left Red Rock. We took my car. The Mastersons' subdivision in Summerlin was only a few miles north of the casino, and we wound our way through rush hour traffic in less than fifteen minutes. I circled around the cul-de-sac at the end of the road and did a quick drive-by of the house.

"Lights are still on," I said.

Carlos nodded. "Somebody's home."

I parked on the opposite side of the street about two houses down. We were out of the way but close enough to get a clear view of the front door.

"Okay, so why are we here?" Carlos asked when I turned off the engine. I had filled him in on the basics, but not much else.

"Okay. One of the keys to the murder trial was Cody's testimony that he and his wife were together on the night of the murder. And she backed him up on it. She said not only were they together, they were having wild sex the whole night."

Carlos nodded. "I remember that part."

"So I came here yesterday with another PI named Mike. Amy was here alone, and Mike went inside to talk. While he was there, he overheard her on the phone planning a long weekend with someone who sounded like a boyfriend," I said.

"So we want to catch her in the act? You trying to blackmail her?"

"Not exactly. I just want to see what the hell's going on with her marriage."

"Gotcha." Carlos turned on his iPod and put in his earbuds. He fished in the backpack he'd brought with him and hauled out a massive business textbook, which he began reading and highlighting with a pink highlighter. I peeked. The pages seemed to be nothing more than squiggles, numbers and Greek symbols. I frowned at him.

"Portfolio theory," he explained.

"Whatever." I shrugged and resumed my blank stare directed at the Masterson house. Within minutes there was movement in the house behind the partially closed blinds. Someone was moving back and forth in what looked like the master bedroom. I figured it was Amy finishing up her packing.

The minutes ticked by and the activity in the house stopped around 6:40. It was still bright out, although the palm trees were casting longer and longer shadows as the sun quickened its descent behind the Masterson house. I had my rear-view mirror turned so I could see any oncoming traffic, but not a single car had made an appearance.

"Quiet around here." I said it loudly enough to be heard over Carlos' music.

Carlos nodded. "People who have houses like this can afford to get out of town for the summer."

Good point. Things remained quiet until about 7:15, when a white Cadillac Escalade appeared out of nowhere in my rear mirror. I slunk down low in my seat as it barreled by and turned sharply into the Masterson driveway. Amy's visitor was in a hurry. I reached in the back seat and whipped out my camera, a digital Olympus with a 15x optical zoom lens.

Carlos frowned. "You and your photos."

"Never hurts to get dirt on somebody. Even if this doesn't lead to anything useful, it might give me a little leverage on her."

Carlos pondered that. "I like your style," he said.

Amy appeared at the door before the driver even put the car in park. She'd been waiting for him, and even from a distance it was obvious she was in a stormy mood. She propped her front door open and began hurriedly hauling a series of Louis Vuitton designer bags out to the Escalade.

The SUV's door opened and the driver got out. "Shit," I whispered.

"What?"

"I know that guy," I said. "See these red marks on my neck? They're from his fingernails." I remembered his name tag: E. Holman. He must be "Eddie."

Holman walked gingerly over to meet Amy behind the Escalade. I chuckled involuntarily.

"What now?"

"See how he walks? He's limping."

"You like to laugh at cripples?"

"I did that. Kneed him right in the nuts."

Carlos made a face. "That ain't right."

"Don't get on my bad side, kid."

Holman pressed a button that opened up the car's massive rear hatch. Inside was a large black leather duffel and a set of golf clubs. Amy's voice was echoing around the deserted cul-de-sac. She was carping that he was late. Carlos took the camera from me and zoomed in.

"She's hot," he announced.

I snatched the camera away from him. "How does your girlfriend put up with you?"

"I work a lot."

I snapped a few more photos. Carlos was right: Amy Masterson was a good looking woman. Blonde, about thirty. Curvy enough but with the skinny, athletic build of a tennis pro. Her round face made her look a little like the Swiss Miss girl. Holman went into the house and hauled out Amy's set of golf clubs.

"Well, it looks like they're fighting, so we're not going to get a shot of them kissing or anything," I said.

"Did you get the golf clubs? That's good enough. They're obviously going away together."

I nodded. "I wonder what she told Cody she was doing for the weekend. Or if he even cares."

They climbed in the Escalade and Holman backed it out. I began to panic. I hadn't appreciated just how high the SUV stood to the ground compared to my little Audi. As they turned towards us, I realized Holman would have a clear angle to look down into my car as he passed us. We were sitting ducks.

"Crap," I said. "Carlos, don't get the wrong idea, but I need you to kiss me right now."

Carlos didn't need to be told twice. He lunged towards me. I was aiming for his chin, but he found my lips and locked on. I wrapped my arms around him and held on until the low growl of the Escalade's engine had passed us by. His back and shoulders were amazingly muscular.

"You can let go now," I said.

He was grinning sheepishly. "First she plays hard-to-get, then she's all over me!"

"Yeah, right. I think that means I don't have to pay you for today."

"Admit it. You enjoyed it."

"Dream on." I wasn't going to give an inch. But I admitted to myself that it wasn't a totally unpleasant experience.

I was fixing my hair in the mirror when another car came upon us without warning. It was a low-slung red convertible driven by a blonde man in sunglasses. Before it reached us, I ducked down and pinned my neck against the frame of the door. Carlos was peeking over the dash.

"The car's pulling up the same driveway," he said.

I inched up in the seat and got a look for myself.

I recognized him from the newspaper. "That's Cody all right."

"No wonder she was in such a hurry to get out of there with her boyfriend," Carlos said. "Cutting it pretty close."

Cody parked the car in the driveway, and I looked through the zoom lens. "Damn," I said under my breath. Cody Masterson was easily the best looking man I had ever seen in person. Or anywhere. He was a trim six feet, with longish light yellow hair tucked back behind his ears. He was wearing a thin linen short-sleeved shirt and tight gray pants with black shoes. Work clothes, I guessed. Businesslike, but stylish. He didn't have leading man looks—he was too beautiful to be taken seriously. Cody was more like a soap opera star. The kind of guy who was born to split his time between the gym and the bedroom.

"Look at that butt," I said. I don't know why I said it, but I did.

"It's not bad," Carlos conceded.

I continued admiring Cody through the zoom lens as he walked up to the house. "You have to admit, that man is fine."

"Oh, he's a dreamboat," Carlos lisped in a high-pitched voice.

"Oh, come on. You can admit when another man is attractive. Why are men so touchy about that?"

"Admitting another dude is good looking is the first step on the path to turning *maricón*," he explained. "Everyone knows that."

"That's stupid. You're saying you can't tell the difference between Cody Masterson and Carrot Top?" The comedian Carrot Top always seemed to be playing somewhere in Vegas, which meant that his pasty white face and gnarled red hair were constantly plastered on giant billboards everywhere you looked. I had known people who'd changed their routes to work just to avoid them.

"Carrot Top. Now that's one ugly homey," he said.

"I want to see what Cody's up to. You want to stick around?" I asked.

"It's your money. I'm supposed to work at nine but I can call in. Thursdays in July are usually slow until after midnight."

"Call in," I said.

Chapter 14

"So are we watching Cody for business or pleasure?" Carlos asked.

I smiled. "No reason it can't be both."

"You're not paying me enough for this," Carlos complained.

"That's crap. You leave a pool of drool on the floor every time a pretty girl walks by. I'm allowed to look at a good-looking guy every once in awhile."

I hadn't planned on seeing Cody, but I couldn't resist the chance to learn what he'd be up to over a long weekend with his wife out of town. Maybe he'd be looking for a horny brunette with a convertible and fake boobs. I had to remind myself more than once that he was probably a murderer.

Carlos sighed and opened up his book. I guessed he figured himself for the alpha dog and didn't like the competition. The dusk was turning into evening, and after a half-hour of waiting Carlos was getting antsy.

"I should have brought another book," he said.

"Light's fading anyways. Give him a half-hour. There's no way that guy is staying in and watching PBS tonight. Feel like clubbing?"

"I'm an awesome dancer," he said.

I immediately put that image out of my mind and began daydreaming about dancing with Cody at a nightclub. That helped pass the time quickly. My hunch that Cody would not stay put proved true. The light went on in the foyer and Cody's figure began moving about. He emerged from the front door just before 8:15. The light was much dimmer now, but I could see he had changed his clothes and rearranged or washed his hair. Now he wore a tight fitting white polo shirt with short sleeves that revealed a pair of tanned, muscled arms. His khaki pants looked like linen and fit loosely, in contrast to the shirt, and his bare feet were clad in brown sandals. He carried a medium-sized brown leather bag with him and threw it casually into the passenger's seat of the convertible before getting in.

Cody fired up the engine and cranked up the radio as he backed out of the driveway.

"That's a Bentley," Carlos said.

I rolled my eyes. "No shit."

As Cody drove past I crouched one last time in the driver's seat. I grimaced as a painful twinge ran down my cramped spine. I shook it off and checked the rearview mirror. When Cody was a block away I turned my car around and began following him.

"That won't be a hard car to tail," I said.

"No shit." Carlos flashed a wide, toothy smile.

Cody left the subdivision the same way we had come in, and I guessed that was about the only way out of this tangled web of millionaires' alleys. I managed to keep us a good hundred yards behind the Bentley as Cody wound his way east on Vegas Drive, picking up speed as he went.

"Looks like he's headed towards the Strip," Carlos said.

"Probably one of the clubs. Pure or Rain or one of those places all the cool kids hang out in."

I worried that Cody would be harder to track if that's where he ended up. But as we reached the far north end of Las Vegas Boulevard, Cody surprised me by staying in the center lane and crossing through the Strip. We followed him as he turned south onto Eastern Avenue, closing in on the north end of the Strip resort area. But he tacked east again and headed onto the Boulder Highway in the direction of Boulder City and the Hoover Dam.

"Where the hell is he going?" Carlos asked.

"Good question."

I kept pace with him for another couple of miles and followed him through the darkening suburban streets after he veered off the highway in the suburb of Henderson. He slowed, finally, and ended up turning into a small subdivision. An illuminated sign at the subdivision's entrance read "Westhill Meadows." According to the sign, the development consisted of a single long street with a cul-de-sac at the far end. After Cody turned in, I idled the car near the sign at the entrance. From there we could see that the development still had a few vacant lots with For Sale signs in front. Just like every other development in Vegas. The few houses we could see appeared vacant and unfinished. A couple of bulldozers were parked face-to-face about a hundred feet down the road.

"What the hell is he up to?" I asked rhetorically. "You hungry?"

"I could eat," Carlos said. "Don't you want to follow him?"

"Not now. According to that sign, there's no other way out of that subdivision, and it looks kind of deserted. I'm afraid he'd notice us if we followed him in."

I looked around and found what I needed—a gas station on the next corner. I pulled into the parking lot and angled my car so that I could keep a clear view of the street leading into Westhill Meadows. I hurried into the gas station to use the bathroom and grabbed a big bag of pretzels. I hoped the manager wouldn't mind if we enjoyed the pretzels while we sat in my car in the station's parking lot.

"This is food?" Carlos asked, eyeing the pretzels skeptically.

"What do you expect, foie gras and truffles? Any activity?"

He shook his head. "That street is dead, dude."

"Don't call me dude."

"Yes, ma'am."

We finished off the pretzels in short order, but that made us both thirsty and I had to run back into the station to grab a six-pack of Diet Coke. Ten or fifteen minutes had gone by when another car pulled into the subdivision. Another soon followed, and by 9:15 we'd counted three more cars turning in. I couldn't see where they were headed, but it was obvious the deserted subdivision was coming to life.

"Somethin's going on," Carlos said.

"I guess it's safe to go in now. We won't stick out like a sore thumb with all those other cars in there."

We pulled out of the gas station and into Westhill Meadows, and I crept my car past a series of new homes in various stages of construction. The homes looked naked without any landscaping or trees around.

"Nice houses," Carlos said admiringly.

By most standards the houses were large and luxurious, but they seemed kind of blah after our visit to the Masterson chateau in Summerlin. We crept along the road until we found a clump of cars parked at the end of the street. Some were parked on the road and two were in the driveway of a big ranch house that looked like it was the only completely finished house on the street. The red Bentley was nowhere to be seen.

"Where the hell did he go?" Carlos asked.

"Well, either we lost him somehow, or he pulled into that garage."

As we rolled slowly by the house, it became obvious from the loud music that some kind of party was going on. I circled around the cul-de-sac and parked in the crushed stone driveway of a half-built house across the way. I turned off the car and killed the lights just as a tan Volvo pulled up to the party house. The driver parked on the street and got out of the car, a bottle of wine in his left hand. His movements seemed tentative, as though he wasn't sure he was in the right place. There was still enough light to see that he was tall and lean, and when he reached the well-lit front door I could tell that he was somewhat younger, probably mid-twenties, and appeared very well-built. The door opened as soon as he rang the bell, but the visitor blocked our view of whoever had let him in.

Within minutes, two other cars pulled up more or less simultaneously. They parked in front of the house next door, an unfinished colonial with a Dumpster outside, and when the drivers got out they greeted each other like old friends. I couldn't see their faces, but both men were fashionably dressed and abnormally fit.

Carlos chuckled softly. "It looks like an Abercrombie & Fitch employee party."

We waited another twenty minutes, but no more cars showed up.

"What now?" Carlos asked.

"I think Cody's car is in the garage across the street, which means he's hosting a party of some kind."

"Only one way to find out." Carlos found the button on the side of the passenger seat and reclined his chair backwards. He tilted his White Sox cap down over his eyes and began fake-snoring loudly, like in the cartoons. I could almost picture the ZZZZZZZ's emanating from his head.

"What exactly am I paying you for?"

"Hey, this was your idea."

I couldn't think of a better option, so I decided to get out of the car and check out the party myself. Carlos handed me my camera as I got out.

"You're so helpful," I muttered.

Like a lot of Nevada homes, the house's "lawn" was a bed of small crushed rocks rather than grass. Luckily I was wearing comfortable sandals. I moved quickly towards the back of the house, where the action seemed to be, but the loud music abruptly shut off before I got there. I froze. I worried that in the silence people would hear the small rocks crunching loudly underneath my feet. Soft voices began murmuring in the back yard. I eased myself behind a wispy shrub against the house's stuccoed wall and listened for any sign that I'd been seen or heard. All clear. After a minute I began slowly crunching my way to the back of the house.

Behind the house was a large black rail fence, buttressed by thick juniper shrubs at least ten feet tall. Their root balls were still exposed from recent planting. Privacy at any expense, I guessed. More voices bounced around the backyard. Soon there was laughter, and the unmistakable sloshing sound of water being splashed. It was a pool party. Someone turned the music back on.

I tried to find an opening to peek through the shrubbery. I had no luck until I reached the far right corner of the pool enclosure, where the right angle of the fence and junipers allowed a narrow but clear view into the pool area. The pool was lit with several fake Tiki torches and lights that shone up from inside the pool itself. It was larger than I would have guessed. On my right, all I could see at first was a diving board at the end of the pool nearest to me, and at the shallow end of the pool near the house three men in their early twenties were playing half-heartedly with a beach ball. Two of them sipped champagne from half-full flutes as they batted the ball around. When they bobbed up in the water, exposing their bare torsos, I could tell that these guys were serious workout freaks. Carlos was right—any of them could work as models for Abercrombie or Calvin Klein. One guy in particular had jet black hair and darker features, and there was something strangely familiar about him. I figured I'd probably seen him on a billboard or something. Or maybe he was just a composite sketch from my dreams.

I couldn't see anything outside of the pool, and Cody was nowhere in sight. As I watched the three guys with the beach ball, I heard what sounded like a sliding door open and close outside my field of vision.

It was soon followed by five or six quick steps and a Tarzan yell. At first I couldn't see what all the commotion was, but the mystery was soon cleared up when a completely naked man cannonballed into the pool right in the middle of the beach ball players. They managed to scatter at the last second, but the splash from the impact erupted a full twenty feet. The cannonballer emerged from underwater with a triumphant smile on his face and chased down one of the others and jumped on his back. He didn't seem to mind either that his bare butt was fully exposed or that his genitals were pressed against the other guy's back.

Holy shit, I thought. So it's *that* kind of party. I suppose I should have figured it out earlier, but it just wasn't on my radar screen.

I reached down to grab my camera when a voice in front of me yelled, "HEY!" My heart skipped a few beats and I froze, certain I'd been caught peeping.

"You're getting us all wet!" the voice shouted in mock protest. That was a relief. I searched for the source of the voice. I hadn't noticed it before, but if I looked down at a sharp angle I could see about half of an oversized hot tub in front of me through the junipers. Inside the tub were three more men, their backs turned to me. Two bottles of champagne and some plastic cups rested next to the tub amid a pile of wet swimming trunks and robes.

I didn't have a view of his face, but I was sure the blonde guy in the hot tub was Cody Masterson. As I crouched there in the bushes, I tried to process what this all meant. I failed. I had no idea what it meant. It was interesting, for sure, but was it anything more than that?

So Cody enjoyed the company of obnoxiously attractive men. So what? That didn't make him a murderer. Hell, if stereotypes were worth anything, it probably made him less likely to be a violent guy. A lover, not a fighter, and all that. But as I crouched there watching the backs of the men in the hot tub, I began wondering. If Cody preferred the company of men, it seemed a bit of a stretch for him to claim that he and his wife were making passionate love on the night of George Hannity's murder. It might be a crack in his alibi, something the jury hadn't known about. It wasn't exactly a smoking gun, but it was something.

I turned on my camera and tried to position the lens through the junipers. I took a few pictures to test the angle, but it was no good—all I could capture were close-ups of the backs of their heads. I would either have to wait for them to move or find another opening.

I decided to play it safe and wait, but I soon got bored. Luckily, after a few minutes the hot tub jets powered on and made a loud racket that gave me some cover to move. I crept along the back of the lot and managed to find a better angle in the opposite corner of the yard. The blonde guy was Cody all right, and he seemed happily buzzed. I snapped four or five pictures of him and the other men in the hot tub, and for good measure I took a few of the naked guys frolicking in the pool. If nothing else, I could blow them up and paste them on my locker at work.

It didn't take a genius to connect the dots: good-looking young guys at a clothing-optional pool party with no women in sight. Still, I didn't have anything more suggestive than Cody sitting in a hot tub. That could be explained away, whereas a photo of Cody *in flagrante* could not. It didn't look like it was going to happen, though: the three guys in the hot tub seemed content just kicking back with their feet poking up out of the water. I was about to leave when one of them climbed out, grabbed a bathrobe, and headed back to the house. It looked like he was getting more champagne.

Cody was left in the hot tub with the other man, a chiseled-faced guy with close-cropped black hair and what looked like a permanent five o'clock shadow. He looked like a model for Gillette razors. He said a few inaudible words and Cody nodded and climbed onto his lap, and both of them now faced me. The Gillette man began massaging Cody's back and neck with his hands. I made sure my flash was off and began snapping photos. After a minute the man wrapped his arms firmly around Cody's chest and pulled him close, kissing Cody behind his ears and on the side of his face. Cody closed his eyes in obvious pleasure. I snapped a few pictures of the two men in action, making sure Cody was clearly recognizable. That was good enough, I thought. I didn't wait to stick around for Act II.

I snuck around the back of the yard the same way I'd come in and found Carlos dozing lightly in my car. I started it up, keeping the lights off, and got us the hell out of there.

"Any luck?" Carlos asked.

"You might say that. Check these out." I handed him the camera and he began scrolling through the photos on the camera's viewing screen. He had to bring the camera close to his face to get a decent view.

"What the . . .?"

"Never been to a pool party like that, I bet," I said. A mile outside of the subdivision I found an empty parking lot off the road and pulled over. I dug my laptop computer out of the back seat and hooked up the camera to the computer, bringing up the pictures on my computer screen to get a better view. There was no mistaking Cody's identity or his amorous actions.

Carlos shook his head. "I guess that explains why we didn't see any women going in," he said, chuckling. "So both Cody and Amy have boyfriends. Now what?"

"I have no freaking idea," I said, "but it's pretty damned weird, isn't it?"

We drove in silence for most of the trip back to the Red Rock Casino, where Carlos's car was still parked. When we hit a long stoplight I asked Carlos the question I'd been turning over in my head.

"So let's say you're on the jury," I said.

"Okay."

"And Cody and Amy get up and testify that they were having passionate sex on the night of the murder. That's their alibi."

"Okay," he repeated.

"And then you're shown the pictures I've taken tonight," I said. "Do you believe their story?"

He paused to consider the question. "Depends. You mean knowing only what you just said? It's fifty-fifty. The fact that they're screwing other people now doesn't necessarily mean they weren't together then. And maybe Cody likes both men and women."

"True. How about with all the other evidence in the case, though? The financial motive. The murder weapon in his backyard."

"Then I don't believe a word of it," he said confidently.

"Good," I said.

He was quiet for a minute before he piped up again. "You know what else? It probably means you could show that Cody didn't marry Amy for love. She leaves for the weekend and an hour later he's in the tub with some naked dude. That means he probably married her only to get at her casino money."

I nodded along with Carlos. "So if he'll marry someone purely for money, it's not a stretch to think he'd go to other extremes for money as well."

"Like blowing off his brother-in-law's face." Carlos smiled broadly, clearly pleased with himself.

"You just earned your paycheck for the night," I said, grinning. I thought about patting him on the leg, but I didn't want to give him any ideas.

I dropped Carlos off and made we made arrangements for him to track down the Indiana bachelor party again tomorrow. They had seemed pretty tame, and I wasn't worried about watching them every minute of their trip. Heck, they were such lightweights that I might even refund part of Mrs. Finley's check.

On my way home I ran through the night's events in my head. I had started out only wanting to see if Amy was actually cheating on Cody. But I now had damning photos of both of them straying off the reservation, and pretty seriously too. It wasn't the strongest evidence in the world, but it could create enough doubt about his alibi that a jury might find him liable for George Hannity's death and make Rachel a multimillionaire. I thought I would run it by Jeff Katz first, though. After all, he was the guy who'd have to prove it in court.

But even as I patted myself on the back, I couldn't shake another feeling lurking in the back of my mind. I hadn't ever spoken a single word to Cody Masterson, or whatever his real name was, but there was something about him that made me question whether he was the type of person who would kill another man in cold blood. I knew it was purely superficial, but I couldn't get past his looks. He seemed like the kind of guy who was destined to spend his days in satin sheets wearing red silk boxers with hearts on them. A tray of chocolate covered strawberries would be within easy reach. And it wasn't just his soap opera looks. There was something in his manner that seemed basically gentle, even passive. He was a seeker of pleasure, a playboy. I was beginning to see how a jury might have had its doubts that he was a brutal killer.

Chapter 15

The weeknight valet at my building, Vladimir, made my skin crawl. After dropping Carlos off, I had no stomach for dealing with Vladimir's attitude and dirty looks. Why couldn't there be a cute little Tommy clone on duty twenty-four hours a day? What did my six hundred bucks a month in condo fees go for, anyway? I decided to skip the valet.

I pulled into the garage and stretched my legs when I got out of the car. I headed for the elevator, which had a bad habit of always being on the floor farthest away from me. On the way up I decided it would be a good idea to turn on some Wagner and pop open a bottle of Bollinger champagne I'd been saving. It was a special occasion, after all: for the first time since I started I actually felt like I had some useful information on the Masterson case. If nothing else, I had substantial dirt on the key suspect and his only alibi witness, and you never knew where that could lead. I wasn't above threatening to expose one or both of them if it meant Rachel could pay off her debts.

My apartment was three doors down from the elevator. When I opened the door, I could immediately tell something was wrong. My skin began to prickle. My heart rate ratcheted up, and I looked around expecting some creepy burglar to jump out at me. But nothing happened. I flipped on the lights next to the door and surveyed the room. Nothing looked out of place. I threw my keys and phone on the table and tossed my purse on the floor.

I breathed a sigh of relief. False alarm. I must have been hyped up from snooping around all evening, and downing four Diet Cokes probably didn't help. I began filling the soaking tub and threw a little ball of goop in there to make it smell like lavender. The champagne was in a half-crate I stored under the bed. I sat on the bed, took off my shoes, and began to rethink my plan. I decided I didn't feel like drinking warm champagne in a hot tub in July in the desert. Bollinger wasn't cheap, after all, and I didn't want to waste it if I wasn't fully into it.

Plan B wound up being a cold bottle of Corona Light from the fridge. Make that two bottles. I chugged half a bottle and brought both bottles to the bathroom and set them next to the tub. The tub was half-full already, but it would still be another few minutes. I stripped off my clothes and put on the comfy blue robe I'd had since college. I pulled out Wagner's *Parsifal* and turned my stereo up so I could hear it over the noise of the tub.

I inspected myself in the mirror and found the red marks on my neck were slowly fading away. It was about time. At Cougar's men paid for the fantasy of perfect bodies and flawless skin, not red and purple welts and scratch marks. I figured those marks had probably cost me a few hundred in tips in the last week.

I grabbed my half Corona out of the bathroom and headed out to my balcony while the tub finished filling up. The desert breeze felt good, and the beer gave me a cozy warm feeling in my torso. I took another healthy chug of beer and leaned over the railing. The traffic on I-15 whooshed by underneath me. A half-mile away, I could see little people walking up and down the Strip, beginning their night's revelries. Paris was lit up beautifully, and if I squinted I could make out a few couples enjoying window-side tables at the Eiffel Tower Restaurant.

It was then that I tried to scream. No sound came out. All I knew was that an immensely powerful gloved hand had wrapped itself over my mouth. The other arm got underneath my left shoulder and behind my neck, freezing me in a kind of half-nelson. I couldn't move. I squirmed and flailed, but the man behind me had me pinned to the railing. He pushed himself against me. The smell of his big leather glove filled my nose, and I realized then that he was trying to suffocate me. Pure panic set in as he pressed me harder to the railing. I struggled more and more to suck in air through his massive gloved hand, but his strength and weight were squeezing the remaining breath out of me.

A survival instinct told me the only thing I could do was succumb. I silently sucked in as much air as I could and gradually stopped struggling. I made my body go limp in his arms, hoping he'd let up on his iron grasp of my neck. Through some miracle, he bought it. He squeezed himself against me once more for good measure and then held me up straight. He had let go of my neck, but he was still pressing against me with his whole body. A sicko, for sure. Sure enough, he shifted his weight a bit and took one of his gloves off, probably to undo my robe and get a better feel of my body. When he shifted a bit to free up his other hand, I knew I had a tiny opening. In one motion, I twisted out of his grasp and with all my remaining strength I clocked him on the side of the head with my Corona bottle. He never saw it coming.

He let out a low roar and stumbled to one knee, holding his face with both of his hands. A mixture of blood and beer foam poured out between his fingers, but I didn't stick around to play nurse. When our eyes met, I saw something eerily familiar, but with his bloody hands covering half his face I couldn't quite place him. I bolted from the balcony and ran for the door. He was still making animal noises, and I didn't look back. I grabbed my car keys and phone from the table in the hallway and flew straight out the door.

I was still huffing it when I got to the elevator. By some kind of miracle, it was still on my floor, right where I'd left it five minutes earlier. I jumped in and frantically pushed the button for the garage about a hundred times, as though the elevator would be able to sense my urgency. When the elevator doors finally closed, I found myself staring at a panicked woman in an open robe. I had my phone and keys, but hadn't thought to snatch up my purse from the floor on the way out.

My mind raced. I wasn't going back to my apartment to get my purse, that was for sure. And I knew I was in a bad spot: if I called the cops, it would risk involving them in Rachel's problems, including her drug dealing. By the time the elevator got down to the garage my only thought was to get the hell out of there.

I ran to my car, started it up and gunned it. I pulled out of the garage and turned right, and within a minute I was in heavy traffic on Flamingo Road heading towards the Strip. In front of me lay Caesar's Palace on the left and Bellagio on the right. It struck me that a giant, anonymous hotel might be the perfect place to lie low for awhile and regroup. There just one problem. Even in Las Vegas, I couldn't check into a hotel without an ID or credit cards, both of which I'd left behind in my purse. The light changed, and I followed traffic straight across the Strip thinking that having some kind of plan would be nice.

After I crossed Las Vegas Boulevard I made a left turn, almost at random, into the Flamingo hotel's parking structure. The only coherent thought I formed was that if someone wanted to find me, they wouldn't look for me here. I wound my way up through the dark parking structure and found a semi-deserted spot on the sixth floor.

I turned off the car and tried to calm myself down. The first step was to get some clothes and money. There was a time and place for heroism and self-reliance, but when you're nearly naked and broke you don't have a lot of options. It was time to beg someone for a favor. Who, I wondered, would be least offended by my current state of affairs?

I thought of Carlos first. He'd seen me naked three or four times a week for at least two years. But he would be at work by now and probably couldn't get away. Besides, he'd never let me live it down. And I wasn't sure I wanted to owe Carlos a favor. The rest of my dancer friends would be working by now, too, I figured. I thought of Mike. He'd seen me naked, but I wasn't sure he remembered that he'd seen me naked. It didn't feel right to call him.

An unpleasant sensation began roiling in the pit of my stomach. Somehow my gut knew before my brain did: Jeff Katz would come and help me. He had already seen me nude dozens of times, so there was no issue of modesty if I had to change in front of him. But did I want to owe him a favor either? Screw it. I could kiss him on the cheek and call it even. Plus, I needed to talk to him anyway.

I called 411 and got Jeff's home number. I half-hoped he wouldn't pick up.

"Hello?" First ring.

"Jeff, it's Raven. You're not sleeping, are you?" It was almost 10:30.

"*Raven*, wow. What's up?"

"I need a favor. I'm at the Flamingo. Can you get over here?" I asked.

"Uh, sure. I've got my kid tonight, and a few of her friends are sleeping over, but I think I can trust them."

"You have a kid?"

"She's fifteen," he said.

"Well it won't take too long. I just want you to book a hotel room for me."

"Sounds like an interesting story," he said. He sounded more amused than I would have preferred.

"Also, I need you to get me some clothes. They have a gift shop here. Just a pair of shorts and some kind of t-shirt or something."

"What about panties? And a bra?" he asked hopefully.

I sighed. "That's not necessary. Bring them to the sixth floor of the parking garage. I'm at the northwest edge of the lot."

Chapter 16

Jeff arrived a little earlier than I expected. He pulled up to my car and brought over a pink bag from the Flamingo gift shop.

"I had to guess your size," he said apologetically through the window.

I looked skeptically at the shorts. They were hot pink. "Size 2? Are you insane?"

"They were the smallest ones they had."

"That's all right." It was actually something of a compliment, I figured.

I scooted over to the passenger seat and tried squeezing into the shorts. It wasn't working.

"You of all people should know that I actually have an ass. I think these are designed for ten-year-old girls." Somehow the shorts fit around my waist, but I could feel my butt ballooning out in back. They would have to do for now. I dug into the bag again and pulled out a blaze orange t-shirt that looked like it was sized for a Barbie doll.

"Jeff!" I hissed.

"I thought it'd look good on you."

"Not if it squeezes off my circulation." I got out of the car and contorted my shoulders to try to slip into the shirt. The back ripped open an inch from the neck. At least the tear gave my boobs a little more breathing room. Even with the extra space, they stuck out so much that the shirt didn't even reach my belly button.

"It's a good look for you," Jeff said. "Trust me." He hadn't even pretended to look away while I tried it on, but I didn't care.

"I'm used to dressing like a high-priced call girl, not some cheap whore from the eighties."

"I can go back down and get something else," he offered.

"Screw it. I guess I can wear this for a few minutes. You're the one who has to be seen with me. You can be my john. Let's go check in and I'll explain what's going on."

My laptop was still in my car, so I decided to bring it with us. By the time we reached the lobby I had begun to reconsider Jeff's offer to get me some different clothes. Each step I took made my shorts ride up higher and higher, and my butt cheeks were eventually in full view of anyone who wanted a peek.

It didn't bother me that people were looking. It bothered me that they were getting their looks for free.

Jeff went up to the desk to book a room. I decided to wait for him in the casino, where I stood a chance of blending into the garish carpeting. Luckily Jeff returned before anyone tried to hire me for a quickie.

"We have to go back to the gift shop," I said. "This is ridiculous."

I was used to feeling idiotic, but this was a new low. I managed to select a few pairs of non-pink shorts and a couple t-shirts in my size. I found a couple pairs of Flamingo boxers that looked comfortable, too. Jeff paid for them without comment.

I put my hand out for the room key, and Jeff obliged. "I'll meet you down here in ten minutes," I said.

I managed to scoot into an elevator just before it closed and punched the button for floor thirty-two. On the long ride up I studied myself in the mirrored door. Pink and orange were not a good look for me. I looked like a giant sherbet cone having a bad hair day. I turned around and tried to get a look at my butt. I cringed. It was a miracle I hadn't been arrested.

The elevator doors finally opened and saved me from the grim stream of consciousness my mind had been heading down. I got out and followed the long hallway down to the last door on the end. The door opened on the first try with the key card and I walked in and plunked my stuff down on the floor. The room was a pleasant surprise. Instead of a standard room,

Jeff had booked me some kind of high-roller suite. To the left was a massive sitting area with thick tan carpeting, a small dining set and a pair of leather recliners. In the far corner, two suede couches faced an amazing corner view looking down at the Strip. There was a Jacuzzi tub in the marble bathroom, and two very large TVs. The bedroom was its own separate room. I smiled. Jeff had done good.

I changed into something less objectionable and found Jeff downstairs inspecting a counter of overpriced chocolates in the gift shop. He seemed disappointed by my change of clothes.

"Maybe I'll wear the outfit you bought me for Halloween," I said. "Although usually I don't wear much more than a mask. Anyway, how about buying me dinner? All I've had since lunch was half a bag of pretzels."

"Sure. They have a good café here. Lindy's, a New York deli."

After wandering aimlessly for five minutes, we were informed that Lindy's had closed ten years ago. In its place was a tropical themed restaurant. At this hour it was half-empty, and we found a spot at the counter. The waitress took our orders. Two cheeseburgers, with fries, and two large Heinekens. Jeff assured me they went great with junk food.

"Anyway," I began, "someone broke into my apartment. He was waiting for me on the balcony, and he almost killed me."

Jeff's face immediately became serious. "Wow. I'd say you could come stay with me, but Anna and her friends have taken over the house and . . ."

"No thanks," I cut him off. Not in a million years. "The suite is beautiful, by the way."

"You're worth it. Actually it was free, so don't worry about it. I have a lot of points built up at these places."

"Really?"

"I play a lot of craps." He smiled lamely. "So who was this guy on your balcony?"

"I can't be sure. I didn't get a great look at him. But I'm pretty sure it was a guy from the Outpost. He has sandy brown hair and a mustache, and he's built like a refrigerator. He was one of the guys that was in the back room with me."

"The back room?"

"Oh yeah, I suppose I haven't seen you in awhile. The guy on my balcony and the head of casino security threw me out and banned me from the place. The security guy got a few million of my skin cells under his fingernails."

"Huh." Jeff looked contemplative.

"What?"

"Never mind. I'd just hate to see anything happen to you. Is it worth all this? I mean, I'm sure Rachel will understand if you want to back off. Just call the cops, let them take over."

It sounded so easy. Just call the cops—as if that hadn't occurred to me every step of the way. "I've been thinking about that for the last hour," I said, "but by now I think I'm in too deep to just walk away. These people know where I live, obviously. The cops would come barging in and blow everything. And then Rachel's in the same place she started. Or worse."

"So who are these people?" he asked. "Working for Cody, you think?"

"Could be. I actually ended up following Cody across town and watching him for awhile tonight. He has some interesting hobbies," I added cryptically.

Jeff took the bait. "Stamp collecting? Scrapbooking?"

"Well," I paused. "He likes to host pool parties for lots of other young men." The waitress behind the bar looked over at us discreetly.

Jeff took a second longer to catch my meaning. "No way," he whispered. "He was always surrounding himself with gorgeous women."

"I think that was just a ruse. A cover. He was in that beefcake strip show, remember? It wouldn't be good for business if people learned that the star of the show was more interested in other men than women."

"Wow," was all Jeff said. His food soon arrived and I recounted the evening's events as he chewed his meal. I kept it brief and hit only the high points. Jeff ate like a pig, but his lawyer's mind was working like an elegant computer. He zeroed in on what I thought was the key issue. "Big picture, it sounds to me like Cody was probably not doing his wife on the night of the murder. That was his alibi, right?"

"You got it," I said.

"Well there you go. With that juicy little tidbit about his personal life we could probably nail him in a civil case." He seemed pleased. I wasn't so cavalier about exploiting a man's personal sex life, but it was hard to disagree with Jeff's pragmatic analysis. It was also a relief that my efforts hadn't been a total waste.

"It's just . . . It doesn't fit perfectly together for me."

His eyelids danced in surprise. He was working on a huge bite of burger, so I kept talking.

"I agree, the evidence looks bad for the murder. Like you so eloquently put it, with the pictures I've got it will be a lot harder to convince a jury he was banging his wife the night Hannity was killed."

Jeff came up for air. "Pictures?"

No one else was near us, so I opened up my laptop and ran through a few of the photos for him. He wasn't shy about studying them.

"These guys do not eat a lot of cheeseburgers," he said. "So did anyone know you were going to be out tonight?"

"No. Just Carlos, the bouncer at Cougar's, and that was last minute."

"You think they're watching you?" Jeff asked.

"I don't know. Probably. It's not like I'm hard to follow around."

Jeff chuckled. "So do you think Cody was behind this?"

"I really don't know. I have to assume so, since he's the one with the most to lose and he's running the Outpost. At least, in theory."

"Who else would be behind something like this?" Jeff drained his Heineken and signaled the waitress for two more.

"Well, the general manager, Phil d'Angelo. He seemed pretty pissed off that I would even consider looking into the case. I don't know if he's working for Cody or his own. But he was the one who got me kicked out of the casino. There was one other thing." I filled him in about what Mel Block had told me at the Del Mar racetrack.

"Hmm." Jeff pondered the question. "So if Cody or this d'Angelo guy are skimming off the top, they'd be really interested in putting a stop to what you're doing."

"Right."

"Does Amy know she's being ripped off?"

"Nope. But right now it's just one old man's theory. I have no proof, and I don't think I'm going to get any."

"That stinks. It complicates things. If there wasn't any financial hanky panky going on, you could just follow the trail back up through this guy who tried to kill you."

I wasn't following. I think it showed on my face.

Jeff tried again. "I mean, now you know there could be *other* people who want to stop your investigation, and their reasons for wanting to stop you might have absolutely nothing to do with the murder of George Hannity. It's like you were trying to avoid waking a sleeping bear, but you stepped on a hornet's nest in the process. "

I frowned. "So I nearly got killed, but I didn't even manage to get any useful information out of it."

"Right. There are too many variables. The guy who tried to kill you might have nothing to do with our murder case."

"You have a way of making things so clear," I said, smiling. I burped out loud.

Jeff induced a burp himself and beamed like a proud father. The waitress shot us another look, this one not as discreet as her last effort.

"Seriously, though, you need to stay out of sight. Even if someone followed you here, you're checked in under my name. Hopefully there's only one person who wants to stop you, but you can't safely make that assumption."

Jeff signaled for the check.

"Thanks for meeting me here," I said. "Your daughter and her friend have probably broken into your liquor cabinet by now."

"Yeah," he sighed. "Duty calls."

Chapter 17

It was only 6:30 in the morning, which meant I had gotten all of five hours of sleep, but my mind was racing. After lying in bed another hour, I took a long soak in the hot tub. I was doing my best to ignore my problems, but they kept pressing themselves into my consciousness, so I gave in. After thinking it through, I decided that my most immediate need was to rule out Cody as the one who was behind the assault in my apartment. If that meant he wasn't George Hannity's killer, so be it. Rachel would not be happy. But for the time being I was more interested in who was disrupting *my* life—if it wasn't Cody, I needed to know who it was. Everything else would have to wait.

After I got out of the tub I put in a call to my building and asked security if they could look into how someone had gotten into the building without living there. The morning security guy didn't sound very enthusiastic. A lot of my neighbors had bought apartments before I did, when prices were thirty or forty percent higher. After the market collapsed a lot of people couldn't afford to live there, so they made do by renting them out. Since so much of my building was either subleased or rented out on a weekly basis, new people were coming and going all the time. That was unsettling. Why have building security at all?

I needed food, and I didn't feel like going back to the tropical café. And ever since a high school band trip to Peoria, I'd had an aversion to room service breakfasts. After wandering aimlessly for a few minutes, I found myself in the line for the Flamingo buffet, which proved to be a mistake. It quickly became obvious that I would be waiting in line all morning, and the prospect of standing there behind two-hundred other low-lifes like me was not a pleasant one. Hunger is one of my great motivators, so I decided to stroll casually over to the VIP line as though I had simply forgotten for a brief spell that I was a VIP. The elderly Asian woman guarding the entrance frowned at me, and from what I could gather from her mumbling it seemed I didn't have the specific VIP credentials she was looking for. But I did have a room key and the little cardboard folder it came in, which was enough to show that in fact I *was* very important. Suite 3266 was not for nobodies. The woman grunted something in disgust and waved me through. A lot of people in this town worked for tips. She wasn't one of them.

The first time my younger brother came to visit me in Las Vegas, he professed the sensible view that a Las Vegas buffet should be treated as a kind of informal eating contest. I was hard-pressed to disagree. After all, you paid a flat fee. It was a challenge issued by the chefs: I dare you to eat all this stuff.

My first round consisted of hash browns and greasy sausage, with a cup of putrid coffee on the side. That was the round of satisfaction. In case of nuclear war, power outage, or terror attack, I would have ample energy. At least until lunch. The second round was the novelty round, designed to stock up on things like dates, pickled eggs and Alaskan king crab – the stuff you would never eat for breakfast unless you were at a Vegas buffet. Round three was freestyle. I came back to my table with a waffle covered in whipped cream and chocolate sauce. In a race against the impending sensation of being stuffed, I mauled it with abandon. I'm sure that I had chocolate and white stuff on my face, so I kept my head down until I finished eating.

I came up for air and wiped my face with a handful of napkins. It was then that I realized my stomach had not prepared itself for such an onslaught. It was beginning to make unusual noises, the kind my grandma used to make after polishing off a bowl of figs. I cursed my little brother and his inane theories about buffets. I left the table feeling slightly ill and more than slightly idiotic.

I spent most of the rest of the day in a horizontal position digesting my breakfast and cursing myself for thinking crab legs, brine soaked eggs and chocolate waffles would be a combination my stomach was equipped to deal with. This is how Elvis must have felt all the time, I thought. Holed up in my high roller suite, I flicked on the TV and watched the stock market plummet for awhile. My booking agent doubled as a financial advisor, but he didn't seem to be doing a very good job of it lately. Watching the market reminded me I needed to call him and fire his ass. I could get orthodontist convention gigs on my own.

I considered just blowing the afternoon and sitting in the hot tub with a bottle (okay, two bottles) of room service champagne, but the thought of champagne in the hot tub reminded me I still had to deal with Cody Masterson. Or whoever else wanted me out of the picture. By 4:15 the maids were getting antsy to clean my suite, so I forced myself to leave for an hour. I decided to walk the half-mile to my condo to talk to the security guard.

It was a sweltering fifteen-minute walk. I gratefully escaped the afternoon heat and approached the security stand in the center of my apartment building's marble and glass lobby. The man working behind the desk was young, clean cut and recently shaved, with shiny medium-length black hair. From the look of him, I figured his shift had just started. I introduced myself as a resident and he responded in what sounded like a Russian accent.

"And you were working here yesterday at this time?" I asked.

"Yes, ma'am. Monday through Friday, same time. You are the one who called this morning about a break-in?"

"Yes," I said. I noticed his name tag read "Ivan," and apparently Ivan and the security staff were more on the ball than I'd given them credit for. "Anyway," I continued, "I'm wondering how someone could just walk in here and get into my apartment."

"I am very sorry about that, miss. We have been trying to upgrade our security systems, but there are just too many new residents all the time. It's very possible that the intruder actually sublets a place from someone else. There are a few dozen condos for rent on the internet at any given time. All it takes is money. One month's rent as a down payment."

"So no background checks, no credit checks, nothing."

"I'm afraid not, miss. Actually this was the request of several of our residents, who wanted to have the ability to rent out their places quickly and easily."

"Okay, but how could someone get into my apartment?"

"We've looked into that. Your key is magnetically coded, so he would have needed to get a copy of your key from someone or have it made here in the building."

"Doesn't sound likely," I said.

Ivan nodded. "Probably not. There is another way. Was the intruder an athletic person?"

"Definitely. I was lucky to get away from him."

"Well, it's possible to string a rope from another balcony and climb up or down to get to yours. There's really no way to prevent that."

"I see. Thanks for your help." It looked like I would be spending some more time at the Flamingo.

Ivan asked whether they should file a police report, but I told him to hold off for now. I was trying to avoid creating too many waves, and a bunch of cops sniffing around would probably put an end to my investigation. I thanked Ivan again and took off.

I decided to be paranoid and not head directly to work. If someone was still watching me, I didn't want to make it too easy for them to find me. It was early rush hour, which meant it'd be hard to find a taxi on the street or in front of my building. I decided to head over to Caesars Palace and stand in their taxi line, and on the way I kept an eye out for anyone following me. Getting to Caesars on foot meant darting across several lanes of traffic going in both directions, and that made it almost impossible for anyone in a car to follow me. The taxi line was surprisingly short, and I caught one within minutes and had the driver drop me off at the Thai restaurant near Cougar's.

I sat at the bar and had a small curry pork dinner by myself. I was pretty thick-skinned, but on a Friday night I felt a little self-conscious eating alone. I rushed through my meal and got out of there. I wondered whether I was crazy to dance that night, but I wanted to stick to my normal routine as much as possible. And I hadn't missed a Friday night in years. There's no way I was going to let a little thing like attempted murder allow the younger girls to poach my regulars.

The nice thing about my night job was that I could show up wearing just about anything, including a t-shirt and shorts from the discount rack at the Flamingo gift shop. I kept a few leather outfits and some g-strings in my locker at work, and that would be enough to get me through at least one night.

I was glad I went to work. Three of my regulars were in the house, and one of them wanted to share me with his out-of-town clients. I spent half the night being passed between about eight different Korean men, and each one shoved a C-note at me when I finished dancing for them. Very nice people, the Koreans.

I was exhausted by one, but I didn't get out of there until three. The Flamingo bed proved very comforting, and I slept late into the next morning.

Chapter 18

There's nothing like a good night's sleep to focus my energies and resolve. I had bummed around too much the day before, and when I finally woke around 10:30 I knew immediately that it was time to talk to Cody Masterson. As nice as the Flamingo suite was, I didn't feel like moving in. I was determined to reclaim what had passed for my own life.

I thought everything over during an extra long shower. As Jeff had pointed out, it was possible that more than one person wanted me off the case, or off the planet. If I had stumbled onto some kind a skim operation, that hornet's nest might have nothing to do with George Hannity's murder. Maybe Mel Block had had second thoughts and warned someone about what he told me. Or maybe Amy had tipped off people at the casino that Mike was asking about it. It didn't seem too likely, though. Mel was dying and seemed to be on my side. And as the sole owner of the Outpost, Amy would be the one getting robbed by any kind of inside skim. Either way, it was disturbing that I had almost gotten killed without necessarily making any progress in solving the case.

But it occurred to me that if Cody was behind everything, he was definitely going about things indirectly. He was relying on Phil d'Angelo to shut me down, and d'Angelo was using his security goons at the casino to get rid of me. Somehow, it seemed safer to go straight to the source—Cody himself—rather than try to untangle the web of people involved at the casino level. Cody seemed downright harmless in comparison to d'Angelo, Eddie Holman, and the Brawny man who'd tried to kill me.

Talking to Cody was the kind of thing that had to be done in person. I debated whether to try to find him at his chateau in Summerlin or at his east side party house. His wife was still out of town with Holman, so I figured he'd probably have spent last night at the party house too. I got my car from the Flamingo valet and headed over to Cody's half-built subdivision. On the way I stopped at a pharmacy and had some of my digital photos from the pool party Thursday night made into 8x10's. I studied them for a minute in the parking lot and sighed. Why were all the best looking men gay?

Things in Las Vegas tended to look dramatically different under the desert sun than they looked at night, and I had more trouble than I expected retracing my route from two nights earlier. I eventually found my way, though, and as I approached the house I wondered whether Cody—if he was even there—would be alone. This time there were no cars in the driveway or out front.

I parked directly in front of Cody's house. I had decided the best approach was the one Mike had taken with Amy: pretend I was investigating some kind of embezzlement at the casino rather than the murder itself. There was no sense confronting him about that, at least for now.

I walked up to the front door and rang the bell. Within seconds the door opened and Cody appeared in a white robe and sandals. He was giggling in a high-pitched voice, looking down and fumbling for something next to the door. "I was wondering when you'd notice," he said. When he looked up at me he stopped cold.

"Hello," I said. Obviously he had been expecting someone else. His face looked profoundly confused, as though he had just woken up from a strange dream. He continued to gape at me with uncomprehending wonder, like a baby seeing itself in the mirror for the first time. He said nothing.

"I'm Raven McShane. I'm sorry to track you down like this, but I have some information I'm sure you'd like to hear about."

Still nothing. I wasn't sure if his confusion was due to the appearance of a stranger at his door, or if it was due to the appearance of this stranger in particular. After all, if Cody had ordered me killed, I could see how he might be he might be a little confused by my presence. It was getting more and more awkward as the seconds ticked by. I smiled gingerly as I stood there while he tried to make sense of things. I tried my best to look nonthreatening.

"iPhone," he blurted out. After all the buildup, I had expected something a little more profound.

"Sorry?" I wasn't catching his drift.

He looked sheepish. "My friend Lawrence left his iPhone here, and I thought you were him."

He turned and grabbed the white phone from a table next to the door and made a show of holding it up to me. At least he was speaking in complete sentences now, I thought. But there was still something of the cornered animal about him.

"Mind if I come in for just a minute?" I asked. I whipped out my I.D. and stepped across the threshold. I decided to take advantage of his obvious confusion before he got himself together enough to object. He glanced at my I.D. without studying it. It seemed to perplex him even further.

"Would you have any coffee?" I asked.

"Um, yeah. Regular is all I have." He was still eyeing me warily, as though I was a creature from another planet. I did my best to look like I came from a friendly one.

"Perfect." Regular coffee is what people from my planet drink in the mornings.

While he went to make coffee, I insinuated myself into the center of the house and looked around. It smelled like fresh paint more than anything else. The home was sparsely furnished, but what was there looked like high quality stuff. The living room actually had a fairly masculine layout. Two oversized brown leather armchairs made an L with a massive tan couch, the focus of the room being what looked to be a sixty-inch flatscreen TV and sound system.

Cody shuffled at half-speed and led me into the kitchen, where a faint smell of incense wafted through the air. The kitchen was something of a mess, with a dozen or so champagne and wine bottles clumped together in the corner of a large gray granite counter top. A few store-bought hors d'oeuvres lay uneaten on platters. I wondered whether the mess was from last night or from the party I'd stumbled upon two nights earlier.

Cody methodically began the process of making coffee. He seemed more comfortable now that he had something familiar to do with his hands. He hadn't said anything, and I took a seat on a stool and watched him while the coffee maker began gurgling. He was taller than I expected—I'd only seen him from a distance and half-submerged in his hot tub—and even with only sandals on he appeared about six-one. And despite being disheveled and unshowered, he still looked damned good. I had to remind myself for the hundredth time that he might be a murderer.

Cody kept his focus on the coffee, watching it drip slowly into the pot. The brewing coffee made occasional burping sounds, but the continued silence added another dollop of awkwardness to an already weird situation. I began wondering what was wrong with him. It was one thing to be taken by surprise by an unexpected visitor, but I surprised people all the time. Usually people began acting unsurprised after about five or ten seconds. Cody was either extremely shy—a possibility I dismissed out of hand, since I didn't know too many shy ex-exotic dancers—or something else was going on altogether. Maybe he had pressed a silent alarm and was just biding his time until his henchmen showed up to haul me away and dump me in Lake Mead. I wasn't going to find out just sitting on a stool.

"You're probably wondering why I'm here," I said. Stating the obvious seemed the best course of action. I got up from my stool.

"A little, yeah," he said. The coffee maker spewed out its last noisy burp of steam, and Cody poured us two cups. He turned to face me and made direct eye contact for the first time. When our eyes met, my knees almost gave out, and I grabbed onto the countertop for support. I had heard of women swooning before, but I thought that was something that only happened in Harlequin romance novels. For the second time in as many minutes, I reminded myself of his criminal past. I also remembered that he probably didn't even *like* women. Even so, my hormones obviously didn't make those kinds of distinctions. They were telling me to get him to the bedroom ASAP to begin spawning a dynasty of blonde half-Swedish supermen and women.

When I recovered, I noticed that his deep blue irises were framed in pink rather than pure white. It was finally starting to make sense—I had just been too slow to catch on. Pink eyes, a dazed appearance, strange behavior. And incense. Cody had just smoked up. He seemed baked medium-rare or medium rather than well done, but he was definitely stoned. I was less sure of whether that was going to help me or hurt.

I decided to press on, but I had no idea what I was going to say. "Like I said, I have some information I'd like to run past you that I think you will be happy to hear."

"Okay," he said, taking a larger gulp of piping hot coffee than was prudent. He cringed and made a face like a toddler who'd just touched the stove. "Hot," he announced.

"I don't think you killed George Hannity," I said firmly. It was from left field, but I decided to go with my instincts.

"I didn't," he said immediately, fixing his pinkish eyes on me again. He continued to stand next to the countertop cupping his coffee mug in his hands while I sat on one of the rickety bar stools. I could think of more comfortable places to talk, but I didn't say anything.

"The problem is, I also think you lied to the jury." I was trying to keep my voice soft and nonthreatening.

"Oh," was all he said. Another big gulp of coffee. "Who did you say you were with?" he asked. His first push back.

"I'm on my own, not with anybody. Professional investigator. I'm looking into the Hannity murder, which I don't think you committed, but I need to make sure. I need you to be honest with me." He began focusing intently on my words, as though some red flag was going off in the deep recesses of his mind. He was willing himself to concentrate and shake himself out of his pot-induced haze.

"I thought all that was over forever," he said. "You know, there was a trial and everything. Not guilty."

"I remember. But you probably know that a lot of people still think you did it, and I think I can help you clear your name."

"Why do you want to help me?"

"I'm in the business of helping people," I replied. I hoped it didn't sound too corny. Luckily he dropped it.

"And why do you think I lied?"

I paused a few seconds for effect. "I have reason to believe that you and your wife might not have been together on the night of the murder." I hadn't meant it to sound so cop-like and official.

Now it was his turn to pause. He gulped his coffee again. I sipped mine. It was undoubtedly the worst coffee I'd ever had. Did he forget to use a filter?

"Okay, but you said you know I'm innocent, right?"

"Yes," I agreed. I never said I knew he was innocent, but that was a small point. I wanted to stay on his good side. "It's just that your alibi has some problems in terms of, uh, certain factual discrepancies. If you can work with me on this, we can get closer to finding the actual killer."

"Well I didn't lie," he said. He set his coffee mug down on the countertop and began pacing around the kitchen.

"Of course it's possible you were mistaken about certain dates or events," I said, trying to use a soothing voice. He continued pacing. I didn't want to trot out my photographs of him and his pool buddies because trespassing and snooping around on his property did not exactly fit with the nice-girl angle I was trying to work. I decided to make an educated bluff instead.

"Cody," I began, "I know you weren't with your wife on the night of the murder. The reason I know you weren't with her is that I know you were with . . . someone else." Cody stopped pacing.

"I'm hungry," he said. He opened the refrigerator and began rummaging around. I watched. It looked pretty bare inside: several more bottles of champagne and white wine, a carton of orange juice, and what looked like more hors d'oeuvres. It didn't look too promising, although I knew if Cody had come down with a case of the munchies he could eat just about anything. Sure enough, he pulled out a half-tray of deviled eggs. He vaguely offered me some, but I waved them off.

He ate the first one in two bites, and licked his fingers. He was not at all self-conscious, but self-consciousness wasn't a quality one expects to find in a former male stripper. The second deviled egg met substantially the same fate as the first.

"It's been like three years. Maybe I don't remember anything at all," he said with a half-full mouth. It wasn't a denial, and that was all the confirmation I needed.

"The other person you were with," I said, looking him in the eye, "wasn't a woman, was it?"

He picked out another egg and returned the plastic tray to the fridge. He was still moving deliberately, but I sensed he was beginning to come out of his haze. He reprised his deviled egg routine: two bites, chewing, licking of fingers. I cringed privately.

"Is that against the law?" he asked.

"No, I believe deviled eggs are legal in this state." If Cody caught my attempt at humor, he didn't show it.

"Why is it anyone's business who I was with on any night?" he asked.

Another non-denial. "It's not," I assured him. "But you couldn't tell the jury where you really were that night. You said you were with your wife."

"I didn't kill George, so what does it matter where I was?"

"It only matters because you were trying to prove you were somewhere else at the time he was killed," I said. I think they taught that in Alibi-101.

"But why do *you* care?" he asked. That was the heart of the matter, wasn't it? If I thought he was innocent, why had I shown up at his doorstep unannounced and kill the nice little Saturday morning buzz he had going?

"I care because I've had my neck gouged, had my apartment broken into, and was a few breaths short of being strangled to death. I thought there was a good chance you could have been involved in those things, which is why I'm here." I didn't raise my voice, but I was getting a little tired of the nice girl approach.

"Well I don't know anything about that," he said calmly. He wasn't fidgeting or pacing anymore. I decided he was either telling the truth or an Oscar-caliber actor.

"Supposing I believe you," (at this, Cody flashed a pained look) "how would you like to clear your name?"

"I thought I already did that," he said, pouring himself another cup of coffee. "Everyone thought I was guilty, but the jury didn't, and they spent weeks on the case. My lawyers said the state spent more than a million dollars trying to prove me guilty, but it didn't work."

"I'm sure you know better than I do that a helluva lot of people still think you did it," I said.

He sighed. "That's their problem, I guess. I can't help that. Look, you seem like a nice person, but this isn't the best time. I've got to clean up and stuff. Can we meet for lunch or something some time?"

"Fair enough," I said. He was trying to get rid of me, but he was being nice about it. "Monday work for you?"

"I think so," he said. Translation: forget it.

"I'll call you. You have a card or something?"

After a short search he found his wallet, fished out a card and handed it to me. I scanned it quickly: "Cody A. Masterson, President, Outpost Casino and Resort." *Resort*, I thought. That was rich. I tried not to guffaw. "You have a cell number?" I asked.

He frowned. It was obvious his buzz was wearing off, and he was becoming more cagey by the minute. I didn't want to piss him off too much. "Look, we have some serious things to talk about," I said. "I'm not just going to go away. I'm trying to help you."

"Okay," he said. He found a pen and wrote down the number on the back of his business card. We shook hands before I left, and I gave him my own card. On the whole, Cody hadn't sounded too enthusiastic about the whole business, but I left pretty convinced that he wasn't guilty of the murder after all. If I had to explain it to Rachel or Jeff, I probably couldn't. It was more of a gut feeling than anything else. But it wasn't my job to prove anything—I was just in the evidence gathering business, and the photos I'd taken were going to count for something. The fact that he might actually be innocent didn't mean a jury wouldn't award Rachel millions in damages. It was just money.

Chapter 19

Carlos told me he was busy that weekend, so I spent a few hours on Saturday afternoon and part of Sunday morning keeping tabs on Richard Finley and his bachelor party. They were Boy Scouts. Finley and his friends gambled a little more and made it to a showing of Jubilee!, the famous topless cabaret show, except that they went to the matinee version that *wasn't* topless. People had a right to be squares, I granted. But then why would they pick Las Vegas for a bachelor party? It made no sense. But I kept these thoughts to myself when I called Barbara Finley to report back around lunchtime on Sunday. She was thrilled that her husband had behaved himself during the whole trip. I headed down to the drug store and printed out a few photos of the bachelor party group, just to prove I'd actually done my job. I sent the photos and a partial refund check of $1,000 to Barbara's work address. Richard seemed like a basically decent guy (apart from lying to his wife about going to Vegas), and I actually felt a little bad that he was going to be in the dog house as a result of my photos.

By Monday morning I was getting accustomed to my high-roller digs at the Flamingo. Too accustomed. Having a maid clean up every day made me understand how some people could actually live in hotels. I also understood how people got soft. After flailing around in my soft bed for the better part of an hour, I got into the tub and dumped in an entire bottle of fragranced goo that made the entire bathroom smell like a steamy flower shop. Unfortunately, I knew, I couldn't sit in the tub forever. Jeff might have a lot of VIP points at the hotel, but I'm sure he didn't plan on blowing them all on me.

I was trying to hide from my growing sense of unease that Cody Masterson might actually be innocent of the murder of George Hannity. If I was right about that, it meant he wasn't the one trying to have me killed, either. And that meant I now had two major problems instead of one. If things panned out as I thought they might, I'd have failed my client and endangered my own life in the process.

My cell phone rang and forced me out of the tub. It was Mike, and my first thought was to invite him over to join me. I decided to resist. I hadn't told him about the intruder in my apartment, and for some reason I didn't want to admit that I'd botched the case so badly that I couldn't even go home.

"You'll never guess who just left my office," he said.

"Elvis?"

He laughed. "Amy Masterson."

"What did she want?"

"Me."

"What?"

"It's been a curse my whole life, but some women just find me irresistible."

It was my turn to laugh. "I find that hard to believe," I lied.

"She was a little shy at first, but once I shut the door she was an animal."

"Seriously, Mike. She's not your type. So what really happened?" I liked the fact that he was starting to joke around with me. It was a baby step in the right direction. I worried, though, that if Amy ever discovered the secret of tequila, she'd have Mike eating out of her hand. That was a little secret I wanted to keep to myself.

"She was wearing a push-up bra or something, because . . ." He let the thought remain unspoken. "Anyway, when I left her house last week we kind of agreed to meet up again."

"You didn't mention that."

"Well it was just one of those things you say. You know, 'let's grab lunch sometime' or whatever. I didn't think she meant it. But she did. And she thought it would be more fun to just show up in person rather than try to schedule a lunch date."

"Wow, maybe you're right. Sounds like she's smitten with you. So what did you two lovebirds chat about? Or did you cut straight to the love scene?"

He chuckled. "She was interested all of a sudden in the embezzlement stuff I had asked her about last week. Why was I looking into it? Who was I working for? That sort of thing. But mainly, she wanted me to take her on my desk. And yes, I resisted."

"Huh." Having seen Cody with his boyfriends in the pool, I had solved the riddle of why Amy was looking elsewhere for male companionship. But still. The woman was a horny slut. A damned menace.

I wanted to run things past Mike and get him up to speed, but I wasn't hungry and didn't feel like sitting at a restaurant with him. Against every fiber of my being, I suggested he could take me to a driving range. He jumped at the idea.

I got there early after sneaking in a quick massage. I had ditched the cheap sandals I'd been wearing in favor of some generic tennis shoes I wouldn't be caught dead in. The rest of my outfit was new, too: low slung tan Capri pants and a strapless black top. It showed off my body but actually left something to the imagination. It was what some people called "Vegas casual," which falls somewhere in that gray area between sleek and slutty.

As I waited for Mike at the range, I was bothered by a vague sense that I might be taking things too lightly. After all, my home had been broken into and I was nearly killed. Yet here I was pawing through a bunch of disgusting loaner clubs that looked like they had been through combat. But what was I supposed to do, cower in fear? Leave town? I felt pretty confident that no one had any idea I was staying at the Flamingo, and it seemed like they hadn't yet figured out that I danced at Cougar's. Until I learned what was going on, I was determined to go on living my life as best as I could.

Mike arrived earlier than I expected.

"What's with you?" he asked.

"What?"

"You look like you just won the lottery or something."

"Oh, that." I smiled. "I had the best massage a few hours ago. This guy at the Flamingo is incredible. Usually the male masseuses have something to prove, you know, to show you how strong they are."

"Maybe they overcompensate because they work in spas," Mike suggested. He put his bucket down in the stall next to mine.

I ignored his little jibe. "I don't know, but I already made another appointment with Eduardo for next week." I bent over my ball and promptly whiffed at it.

Mike stifled a chuckle. He made a show of stretching his back and arms while I pretended not to watch. While he was preening I decided to fill him in on what had happened.

"It's not worth it," he said simply. "I don't care if you're charging a thousand bucks an hour. It's not worth risking your life for a client. This is just about money, after all."

He was right, and I knew it. Even so, I wondered what other options I had. "But it's not like I can just call up Rachel and say 'I quit'. They know my name. They know where I live. I'd have to leave town entirely."

"And you don't have enough to get the cops involved?"

"I talked about it with Jeff Katz, the lawyer who works for my client. I think the guy on my balcony was a security goon from the Outpost. He had a mustache. Looked kind of like the guy on the Brawny paper towel rolls. But I can't be sure. He was covering his face when I got my only look at him."

Mike's eyebrows were raised. "Why was he covering his face?"

That was part of the story I'd skipped over. "Well, I kind of clubbed him over the head with a beer bottle. He was bleeding pretty badly."

Mike smiled for the first time. "Good girl."

He took out his driver and cranked one to the 275-yard marker.

"Still not impressed," I said.

He ignored me and swung again. Same result. "So you think Cody Masterson is behind all this, pulling the strings?"

"I was just getting to that. In short, no. You can laugh and call it women's intuition or whatever you want, but I talked to him and I don't think he did it."

"Did what, the murder?"

"Right."

"Wait, you *talked* to him? When? How?"

"I just went over to his house on Saturday morning. He was pretty stoned, actually, so I think he was being honest."

Mike seemed befuddled. "What chapter of your Detective 101 textbook told you to just waltz up to a murder suspect's house and have a chat with him?"

I grinned. "I kind of make it up as I go along."

Mike scratched his chin and frowned. He was at a loss for words. After a few seconds he tilted his whole head backwards and let loose with a long, rumbling chuckle. "That must be the understatement of the year."

I grinned. "The problem is, that leaves about two million other people in this town who could be trying to stop me."

"That's comforting," he said. "What about what the old guy told us in San Diego? Maybe the whole security staff was robbing the place blind and they killed Hannity to keep it quiet. It would make perfect sense that they don't want you poking around. All it would take is for one of them to get wind of what you're up to."

I nodded. "That's about the best theory I've got at this point. It won't make Rachel very happy, because she wants to nail Masterson and get a judgment against him. But at this point I'm more concerned with nailing whoever's trying to kill me. And I've got to assume that he—or they—are the same ones who killed George Hannity."

Mike was looking thoughtful again. "How sure are you about Cody?"

"You mean about his innocence?"

"Yeah."

"I'd say sixty, seventy-five percent. Why?"

"It's up to you, obviously. But if you think he's in the clear, why not have him help you out? I mean, he's the boss over there, right?"

I nodded. "Technically he's the boss, yes. President. But it doesn't sound like he has much day-to-day control. But I see what you mean. If Cody's not the enemy, he's one hell of a good source of information."

Mike looked serious again and swung. He turned to face me, proud of himself. "It's risky, for sure, but you've already talked to the guy in person. Seems you're pretty fearless."

"I like a challenge," I said. I tried to give Mike a sultry and suggestive look, but I probably just looked idiotic.

Mike and I left the range around 7:15, before I could injure myself or anyone else. I needed to pick up a few things from my condo, and I didn't feel safe going there alone in case someone was still watching the place. Mike agreed to meet me there.

I found my apartment in about the same condition I had left it. Out on the balcony there were no signs of a struggle. The blood was cleaned up, and there was no broken glass anywhere. Someone had turned the faucet off and drained the tub. The idea that someone would come back and clean up the place was almost as disturbing as the break-in itself.

"Nice place," Mike said. He seemed vaguely bothered by it, the way he'd reacted when he saw my new Audi. He had to know I couldn't afford the car and the condo based on my paltry detective business alone, but I hoped he wouldn't ask too many questions.

I found a grocery bag in the kitchen and stuffed it with clothes. I found my purse and wallet untouched. I also dug out the file folder I had begun putting together on the case, which included a stack of printouts of news stories, the trial transcript, and a few notes I had made along the way. No sense leaving that where anyone could get to it. It was eerie being back in there, and we left as soon as I was packed up.

I told Mike I could get back to the Flamingo by myself. He wasn't giving off any signs that he wanted to come with me, although that was nothing new for him. I decided not to look desperate, so I just said goodbye and thanked him for letting me watch his rear end while he swung at golf balls.

When I got back to my room I put my bag of clothes on the floor and set the file folder on a table in the corner. I plopped down on my bed and immediately regretted not inviting Mike in. It wasn't even eight yet, and I was wired. Wired, and a little freaked out after returning to my apartment. Actually, I was a lot freaked out. I think I had been living in some advanced stage of denial, but when I saw my balcony again it had all come rushing back. And there was something distinctly creepy about the idea of someone returning to my apartment to clean things up.

In short, I didn't feel like being alone. I took a chance and dialed up Rachel. I hadn't wanted to worry her or make her feel guilty for what had happened to me, but I didn't feel like calling anyone else. She was free.

"Wow," she said when we got into my room. "You wouldn't expect this kind of room in a place like this."

"Snob," I said, laughing.

"You're right. In the old days, the Flamingo was where the real high rollers stayed."

I'd told her to bring a bottle of something, and she wowed me. "This is like four hundred bucks a bottle." Over the years, a few of my best customers had invited me out with their groups of friends and business associates, as though I were some sort of low-rent geisha. In the process, I'd managed to develop a decent appreciation for champagne. Or at least an appreciation for how much different champagnes cost. Krug 1998 was no slouch.

"George didn't leave me too much of his money," she explained, "but the wine cellar is still *very* well stocked. Luckily the guys I owe money to don't know about it yet."

"Good vintage," I said. I was talking to an empty room. Rachel had disappeared into the bathroom, probably to inspect the tub. She emerged and came over to the windows to take in the view of the Strip.

"Damn," she said. "Nice view."

"So how are the goons? They keeping their hands off you so far?"

"For the moment. I threatened to call in the feds and cut a deal, and that seems to have cooled them off. But I got a voicemail today saying I have to come up with the money by next week."

"You could always move in here with me," I offered.

While I was uncorking the bottle she began pawing through my case folder on the table. At least she'd know I had actually been working on the case, I figured. I hunted around the room and found the champagne glasses in the mini-bar cupboard. The champagne smelled vaguely like fresh-baked McDonald's biscuits, which was a fantastic thing.

"Ooh, he's cute," she said to no one in particular. She was holding one of the newspaper stories I'd printed off the internet.

"Hmm?"

"Nothing. I forgot about this guy."

"Who?"

She sighed. "This guy on the jury was a real honey," she said. I sidled up behind her and handed her a glass of champagne. She took the glass and handed me the printout she was looking at. Since the trial had been one of the biggest local stories of the decade, the newspaper had written a profile of each of the jurors. I'd glanced at the story a few weeks ago but never got around to reading it. I flipped through the pages. There was a short bio of each of the jurors next to a medium-sized head shot.

Page four showed a guy who definitely qualified as a honey, even on my grainy black and white printout. "Is that the cute guy?" I asked.

She nodded enthusiastically and took the story back from me. "Yummy," she said.

"The guy or the champagne?" I asked.

"Both," she said. She took a healthy slurp from her glass.

"Let me see that again."

I looked carefully at the photo. It hadn't jumped out at me right away, but I was sure I recognized the young guy shown in the photo from somewhere. And then it hit me: he had been swimming in Cody's pool on Thursday night.

"Fuck," I whispered, clutching the page.

"What's wrong?"

"This guy. I know him," I said. "He knows Cody. He was one of the guys swimming in his pool on Thursday night."

She frowned. "Cody doesn't have a pool."

"Long story," I said. "I assume you didn't know Cody is . . . well, he likes guys."

"You think he's gay?" she asked, incredulous.

"I don't care what he is, but this guy in the photo is friends with Cody Masterson. Good friends. As in, they swim together in the nude. And according to this story, he was sitting on the jury that set Cody free! I thought I recognized him when I saw him in the pool, but I figured he was a model from a jeans ad or something."

I sat down on the bed. My mind was spinning. I supposed it was possible that Cody and this juror had become friends after the trial, but that seemed far-fetched. It seemed a lot more likely that Cody had bribed some court employee to get his friend on the jury. Or the guy had been a total stranger whom Cody had bribed after he wound up on the jury. I turned away from the table and stared vacantly out the huge window at the Strip thirty-one floors below me. It was still twilight, but the sun had receded behind the Bellagio and the lights were just beginning to take on their familiar nighttime glow.

"Wow," Rachel said softly, and then she repeated it. "Wow." She came over and stood close to me. "What does that mean?" she asked.

"I don't know," I said, still staring out the window, "but it's not good." I stood staring out the window for another minute. "It probably means Cody bribed someone to get one of his buddies on the jury."

"Here," Rachel said. She filled my glass to the brim and it fizzed over. I figured each little drop was probably worth about a buck, so I slurped at it quickly before too much spilled on the floor.

I got out my laptop and sat down on the bed. I pulled up the photos I had taken of the guys in the pool and scrolled through them. I showed Rachel the photo of the juror.

"That's him," Rachel said. There was no mistaking it. He was a few years older now, of course, but the shirtless guy hitting a beach ball with his right hand was definitely the same man as the juror in the newspaper profile. "Wow," she muttered again.

I continued the slide show on my laptop. The finale was a few shots of Cody canoodling with his Gillette model friend. Rachel seemed speechless.

She was studying the pictures intently. "I just can't believe it. Whose pool is this?"

"I think it's his. He's parking his car in the garage, anyway. I figure it's a secret hideaway for this whole other life he has."

"Amazing. And Amy has no idea?"

"As far as I know. I haven't talked to her, though."

Rachel topped both of us off again and frowned at the empty bottle. "We're going to need a bigger bottle."

I nodded somberly. I didn't want to think any more about this case. "Room service," I said.

I found the menu and ordered a couple bottles of a more affordable champagne.

Rachel piped in. "Get some cake, too."

"You drove here, right?"

She nodded.

"You're not driving home. Do you have any aspirin?" I asked.

"I have ibuprofen," she said. "You got a headache?"

"Not yet, but you might want to leave the bottle on the night stand. You're going to need it in the morning."

Chapter 20

I woke up surprisingly clear-headed. Rachel lay next to me, bundled in the soft comforter. Only a thin slit of light peeked in between the thick hotel curtains—she must have remembered to close them. Rachel (and three bottles of champagne) had helped me forget about the Masterson case the night before, but things were coming rushing back to me whether I wanted them to or not. I turned the problem over in my head as I stared at the ceiling. Nothing made much sense. One possibility was that one of Cody's pre-existing friends could somehow have been picked at random for jury duty. I dismissed that out of hand. No one was *that* lucky. Another explanation was that the juror and Cody had somehow innocently become friends after the trial. That seemed more likely, but still a long shot.

Unfortunately, foul play made a lot more sense. Cody must have tampered with the jury somehow. Maybe he had found a way of bribing the court clerk and arranging for one of his friends to be selected for jury duty. Or maybe the juror had been selected legitimately and Cody found a way to get to him. I didn't really care how he'd done it. Either way, he looked ten times more guilty than he did yesterday, and I felt a hundred times more stupid for believing he could actually be innocent.

Rachel stirred, and after a quick cup of hotel coffee she washed up and left. I kept looking at the printout of the newspaper profile of Cody's juror friend. According to the article, his name was Paul Gonsalves. He still looked hot, I mused, even though he was probably a crook. Then again, I'd wanted to jump Cody's bones despite the fact that he was possibly a murderer and almost certainly a jury-tamperer. I needed a boyfriend more than ever, I thought.

I decided I wanted to talk to Paul Gonsalves before confronting Cody or anyone else about it. He was not listed in the phone book. Like most people in this town, he probably relied exclusively on his cell phone, which would be unlisted. My high-roller suite came with free wireless internet access, and I did some Google searches on Paul Gonsalves. They all produced lots of interesting but useless information about a tenor saxophone player of the same name who had played with Duke Ellington's band.

I wasn't a big internet junkie, but I was at least aware that dozens of social networking sites existed online, and it seemed like all of the younger dancers at Cougar's had their own Facebook fan pages. They were constantly updating them to let the world know what TV shows they liked, what kind of cereal they had for breakfast, and what their latest hair color was. I couldn't believe anybody cared about such things, but whenever I logged on dozens of people had commented on the most mundane aspects of my friends' lives, and frequently they offered their own insignificant observations as a counterpoint. Sure enough, after poking around for a few minutes I found a Paul Gonsalves from Las Vegas on Facebook. I had found my guy. Paul's posts and his photos revealed him to be a vain young man, although any man with his face and pecs could be forgiven for vanity. His info page described his interest in modeling and contained page after page of amateur photos of him in various poses. Some of the poses were suggestive, and all of them were shirtless. His listed his age as 23, and he described himself as "gay / bisexual" and "looking." His interests included reading, hanging out with friends, shopping and dancing. Unfortunately, his page didn't say anything about accepting bribes, conspiracy or obstruction of justice. Beyond that, I learned that he was an atrocious speller and worked at Banana Republic. It was time to go shopping.

In the shower I pondered how to approach things with young Mr. Gonsalves. He seemed the kind of person who might require a soft touch, but I was getting distinctly sick of soft touches. After I showered and dressed, I called Carlos and woke him up. He didn't seem to mind, probably because I owed him about six hundred dollars for his work following Richard Finley around town last week. Even so, I decided to wait until he got in the car to tell him we were going on a mission to the Banana Republic.

I'd never been to Carlos' house, so he had to give me directions. I arrived around 10:45 and was surprised at how run-down Carlos' apartment building looked. It didn't make sense. I knew he made a decent enough living at Cougar's, and lately I had been throwing him a thousand or more a month with odd surveillance jobs. To each his own, I guess. I rang the bell. Carlos emerged slowly, squinting into the bright sunlight.

"Man, this is cruel," he said, grimacing. He pulled down the brim on his black White Sox cap to shield his eyes from the sun. He wore a tight white t-shirt and baggy black pants. Two or three gold chains dangled from his neck. I'd told him to look intimidating, and he fit the bill nicely. He looked like a Hollywood version of a gangster.

"You whine a lot for someone with guns like that," I said, eyeing his 18-inch biceps. "Let's go."

"I worked 'til 3:15 last night, so leave me alone," he whined.

"This'll be easy," I explained as we got in my car. "I just want to talk to a guy, and I want you to stand next to me while I do it." I pointed at his apartment. "Nice place, by the way," I said sarcastically.

He didn't catch the sarcasm. "Thanks. Just bought it in February."

It took a few seconds before I processed it. "You *own* that place?"

"Yeah. Sixteen units, fully occupied. So far, on pace for an R.O.E. of twelve percent."

"Stop speaking gibberish," I said.

"Return On Equity," he explained.

"Of course."

"My other buildings are nicer," he said.

I was impressed, but I decided not to say anything else on the subject since it seemed that everything I thought I knew about him was completely wrong. Carlos kept his eyes closed as we drove back to the Strip, his eyes still apparently sensitive to the bright sunlight. He opened them when I pulled into the valet line at the Venetian hotel.

"Where we goin?" he asked.

"Banana Republic."

"Shut up."

"That's where this guy works."

He made a face. "Dude works at Banana Republic and you need backup?"

He had a point. "He's very well put together," I said lamely. "I just want to be as persuasive as possible." I explained how Gonsalves had been one of

Cody's pool guests on Thursday night and how he had also happened to serve on the jury that set Cody free.

I had checked the Banana Republic company's website before picking Carlos up. There were seven Banana Republics in Las Vegas, three of which were within one square mile of each other, and I thought it made sense to start in that area. Our first stop was the Venetian's Canal Shops. The staff eyed Carlos and me warily. I supposed we made an unusual couple, even in Vegas. It turned out that Paul Gonsalves wasn't working there, but the manager on duty smiled when I asked about him. Occasionally he subbed at the Venetian store, she said, but he normally worked at the Fashion Show Mall a few blocks north. They seemed relieved when we left.

We crossed the street and walked the few blocks up the Strip, past Treasure Island, and took the footbridge across Sands Avenue. The Fashion Show mall was the only free-standing shopping mall on the Strip. It was my favorite. Inside was a mixture of upscale department stores like Saks and countless boutiques and shoe stores. The building's white stone facade gleamed blindingly in the late morning light. Carlos began to mutter again. He was not a morning person.

"Don't you own sunglasses?" I asked.

"I squint," he said.

"And bitch."

The shopping mall was austere by Vegas standards—it could just as easily have been a mall in an upscale suburb of Cleveland or Atlanta. Its air-conditioning was set to frigid, as though the mall was planning to host a hockey game or an ice sculpting demonstration in the atrium. On this Tuesday morning it was mostly deserted, although a few determined women in comfortable shoes lugged department store bags around. We quickly found the Banana Republic, and in the back corner we found Paul Gonsalves. He was listening to an iPod and folding sweaters. He wore a tight-fitting chocolate brown polo shirt and flat front khakis. Around his waist was a bright red cloth belt that somehow worked with the rest of the outfit, and on his feet were loafers with no socks. We were the only customers in the store. He looked up from his folding as we drew closer.

"Can I help you find something?" he asked, directing the question at me rather than Carlos. He was just polite enough to not make a face at Carlos.

"Just browsing," I said pleasantly. "My friend said you're the best salesman around," I added.

"Really? Who's your friend?" He stopped folding sweaters.

"Cody Masterson."

Paul didn't say anything at first, but he managed to eke out a nervous smile. "How do you know Cody?" he asked finally.

"Oh, I know him from a long time ago. From before his trial," I lied. "He told me something very interesting the other day about that trial."

"Oh yeah?" Paul asked. He was trying to sound casual, but it wasn't working. Out of the corner of my eye I saw Carlos begin pawing through a neat stack of about twenty freshly folded burgundy polo shirts, as though trying to find one in his size. He flipped each one over and left them all in a rumpled pile.

"It had to do with an amazing coincidence," I said. "Something about having a pal on the jury that set him free." Carlos moved on to a stack of black V-neck vests and began mumbling something unintelligible to himself. The result was another rumpled pile of seventy-dollar brushed cotton sweaters. It was clear that Carlos was making Paul very nervous.

Paul froze, speechless. His face turned a bright shade of pink.

"You know," I said, "I wonder if you could possibly take a ten minute break and have a quick chat with us." I tried to sound like all we wanted to do was to sell him a subscription to *People* magazine. Paul took another look at Carlos and decided to take me up on my offer.

"I'll just go tell the manager."

The three of us left the store and I led us to a little coffee shop a floor below the Banana Republic. I treated for three espressos. Paul and I sat down at a table. Carlos lingered for a few seconds and then made a show of turning his chair around backwards. He sat down facing us and draped his beefy tattooed arms menacingly over the chair's back. Carlos was a good actor.

I showed Paul my I.D. and got down to business. He remained silent.

"Let me tell you what I'm not interested in," I began slowly. "I'm not a cop. I'm not interested in people going to jail or getting into trouble." I scanned Paul's features for any sign of relief, but found none. "I work for money, and only money," I continued, "and I don't give a damn about what happened in the trial three years ago. You and I know that Cody was innocent anyway," I said. "Frankly," I added, "I would have done the same thing you did." I hoped I wasn't laying it on too thick.

"Okay," he said softly. He exhaled deeply, as though a weight had been lifted. He hadn't yet asked what we wanted with him, which meant he probably knew exactly what we wanted. Carlos made a show of looking bored, which he undoubtedly was.

"All I want to know is how much," I said.

Paul had been looking down at the table. He raised his head up slightly. "How much what?" he asked gingerly.

"How much does Cody pay you for what you did?"

"What?" Paul asked. He was trying his best to sound confused. It wasn't an Oscar-caliber performance.

Carlos leaned in and spoke for the first time. He spoke softly but it was loud enough that Paul could hear him. "I told you, Raven. Easier just to go to the cops."

"Probably right," I sighed.

Paul fell for it. "Okay, look, I got twenty-five thousand then and I get four grand a month now. Is that what you wanted?" he asked. "Anyway, it's not all about money."

"Sounds to me like it is," I said.

"No," he protested. "I get to hang out with them, you know? Parties, clubs, stuff like that. We travel sometimes." He was still looking down at the table. "You're not going to tell him I told you, are you?"

"Why bother? He already told me most of it himself," I lied. Paul looked relieved. "The only other thing I need to know is how he approached you. Did he call you or come to your house or what?"

He leaned forward and placed his elbows on the table to prop his head up with his hands. "It was like three days into the trial, I think," he said softly. "I was at this club called Razor, and was probably drinking a little. And this guy comes up to me and says he wants to introduce me to a friend of his, Cody Masterson. And I was like, wow, awesome. He is so hot. I'd been staring at him from the jury box for three days or whatever. He must have noticed, so he found out my name and I guess he had someone follow me. So we met, and talked, and that was that." It sounded like a great argument for not letting accused murderers out on bond while their trials were pending.

I looked at Carlos, and he nodded ever so slightly. It seemed like Paul was telling the truth. I thanked him and told him to go back to work and warned him not to tell anyone about what we talked about or he would get in trouble with the police.

"Makes sense," Carlos said after Paul left.

"What does?"

"This day and age, you ain't gonna just walk up to some random person on a jury and ask if they'll take some money," he continued.

"True."

"That's a felony, right? To take a bribe, you'd either need a lot of money or have some other reason to do it. A personal reason, like sex. Twenty-five G's ain't enough by itself," he said. "Not for me, anyway."

"How much would it take?"

"A million, maybe two. Depending on the case. And no sex predators or serial killers, you know, just something where a guy maybe made a big mistake one time."

I chuckled. "It's good to have principles." Most men probably had a price, I figured, but few would admit it. "So you think Cody picked Gonsalves as an easy target?"

"Did you hear the way he was talking about him? It sounded like he would have done whatever Cody wanted for free. Just to be able to hang out with those guys. That kid is in *into* your friend Cody in a big way."

"Kid? He's *your* age!" I wasn't sure, but I figured Carlos had to be about twenty-four.

"Whatever."

"So Cody seduces him, which wasn't hard, and then provides him enough cash so he can enjoy the finer things in life even though he folds clothes for a living." The kid's story made a lot of sense.

"Wonder how Cody comes up with the four grand a month," Carlos said. "I'm gonna guess his wife doesn't write the checks to pay off her husband's boyfriend."

I laughed. "You should get your own PI's license."

"No way. Money's no good," he said. I took the comment as an unsubtle reminder that I owed him money. I downed the last bitter drops of my espresso.

"I told you about the guy in San Diego, right?"

"The old dude with the hot girl working for him?"

"That's the guy." Carlos had a knack for remembering the key details. "He thought there was some kind of financial stuff going on at the casino. The numbers weren't quite adding up the way he thought they should, and after he left they started sending him a pension he wasn't expecting."

"Um hmm."

"Just thinking out loud," I said.

Carlos nodded. "Could be a nice pot of money that Cody's been dipping into himself," he said. "If it's worth paying off a guy to keep quiet about . . ."

"It's worth killing for." We both stared out at the endless expanse of the mall—white marble and glass as far as the eye could see.

"Well, we know Cody's getting a lot of money from somewhere, and it's been going on for years," Carlos said. "Think about it—he's paid Gonsalves two hundred grand since the trial. And we know the old dude thought someone was ripping off a lot of money from the casino," he continued.

"It adds up. Plus, he's got to fund his little bachelor pad somehow. Brand new homes with pools aren't cheap."

We sat there at the tiny table in silence.

"This case is frustrating," I finally said. It was the understatement of the year.

Carlos was thinking about something. "Would you bribe someone on a jury even if you were innocent?"

I thought about that for a second. "That's the question, isn't it?"

"*I* would," he said, answering his own question. "I mean, I might. If it looked bad. System ain't perfect. It's just something to think about. Messing with the jury doesn't mean you're guilty."

"Thanks, professor," I said. "It doesn't look good, though, does it?"

"Nope."

"Either way, it means he has to talk to me."

Carlos nodded. "Gonsalves is a bargaining chip," he said. "A big one."

I smiled. We were on the same wavelength. "Nothing like having evidence of a felony to get a man to talk. Can I borrow you this afternoon, too?" I asked. Carlos hesitated.

"My girlfriend's watching my kid. She's got to go to work."

"You have a kid?"

"You're a detective?" He sighed and shot a feigned exasperated look up at the ceiling. At least I think it was feigned.

I felt idiotic, but that was nothing new. "I think we need to go talk to Cody right away, before he finds out from somebody else how much we know. It didn't take much to get Paul to talk with us, so who knows what he'll tell Cody."

Carlos sat still, as though posing for an ice sculpture.

"One hour, maybe two," I said. "Two hundred bucks."

He didn't say anything.

"Two fifty."

"Kid goes through fifteen diapers a day. They're expensive," he said.

I had the distinct sense he was working me over. "Okay, let's go. Three hundred is all I can do." I got up and left, hoping Carlos was coming with. He was.

Chapter 21

We stepped outside into what had become an even hotter and brighter day. Directly across the street, the bronze panels of the Wynn resort complex glowed rust orange in the sunlight, as if burning from within. It was the beginning of the lunch hour, and the sidewalks flowed with bustling conventioneers wearing corporate polo shirts with large name tags dangling from straps around their necks. They moved in packs of threes and fours, all on the prowl for the best meal their expense accounts could buy.

We stood on the corner next to the mall in a large open plaza dotted with carts selling sunglasses and t-shirts. Salesmen were hawking timeshares to anyone naïve enough to stop and listen. In the corner, next to the street, were a dozen or so display boxes stuffed with flyers and color pamphlets advertising women you could hire as escorts. I got out my phone and dialed the number Cody had written on the back of his business card. There was no answer, and the voicemail of someone named Phil Ebert kicked in. *Shit*, I muttered. I hadn't thought to check the phone number, but I should have. Writing down a bogus number was exactly the kind of thing a half-stoned guy might do when trying to rid himself of a stranger asking a lot of questions.

I was pissed. "Let's find some cover," I said.

Carlos and I found a small rectangle of shade under the wide awning of a tourist information stand. I paced in and out of the sun for a few minutes trying to figure out what to do. Carlos lost interest and wandered off. I decided to take a chance and call Cody's work line. A woman answered, sounding friendly. Mr. Masterson was in the office, she said, but he was in a meeting. I could make an appointment if I wanted. I said no. The casino had about a thousand security cameras, and I'd be pretty noticeable. I figured I'd get beat up long before I even got close to Cody's office. I thanked her and hung up.

There wasn't much at this point that I was certain of. But I knew three things. First, I needed to talk to Cody Masterson. Second, the Outpost casino was only two blocks away. Third, I had just rented Carlos for the afternoon. A crude plan began forming in my mind.

I found Carlos busying himself with a glossy color pamphlet proudly advertising "Nevada's Nastiest Women." There was a large XXX on the cover. The XXX was stamped diagonally across a color spread showing a dark-haired woman wearing leather and wielding some kind of billy club menacingly at a blonde woman in white. The blonde was supposed to look like an innocent, but she looked just as trashy as the brunette.

"Carlos."

"No way," he said. He didn't look up from the magazine.

"What?"

"I am just along for the ride, man," he said. "Nothing else." He was reading my mind.

"How would you like a quick makeover?" I asked. That wasn't what he was expecting. I explained the gist of my half-baked idea, and he surprised me, first by listening patiently and then by going along with it. We headed back inside the mall and made our way to the Macy's men's department.

On the way to Macy's we passed Saks Fifth Avenue. Carlos nudged me encouragingly as we passed.

"No," I said. Carlos pretended to pout.

At Macy's I bought Carlos a long sleeved white oxford shirt. That would cover up his tattoos, at least. I also got him a pair of navy slacks and a black leather belt. He had jet black basketball shoes on, and I figured they would do. Carlos looked good. He shoved his other clothes into the Macy's bag and handed his Sox cap to me for safe-keeping. He spent about five minutes fiddling with his hair in the mirror.

We walked the two blocks up to the Outpost and found the employee entrance on the north side of the building. There didn't appear to be any key card required, and no security was visible inside. The hallway behind the entrance made an L, and I guessed there was a reception or security desk involved somewhere along the way.

"Tell anyone who asks that you're there to see Mr. Masterson," I said. "It's urgent and involves a close friend of his, Mr. Gonsalves. That should be enough to get him to see you. When you get in, tell him I'm outside and we need to talk immediately or I'll go to the cops about what Gonsalves told us. Got it?"

He looked at me skeptically.

"What's the worst that could happen?" I asked.

"They could kill me and bury me in the desert."

"Bah," I chortled. "The chances of that are less than fifty-fifty."

Carlos grunted and went inside. I moved about fifty feet away from the door and made sure to turn my back to the security cameras watching over the parking lot. I felt awkward standing alone in the parking lot, so I dug out my phone and played hearts against the computer. As usual, the computer was cheating.

My back was turned when I heard the door shut and I spun around to see Cody Masterson emerge accompanied by the newly preppified version of Carlos. Neither looked excited to be reuniting with me.

"You could have called me," Cody said. He was dressed in a navy pinstripe suit and crisp white shirt with a ruby red pocket square. Without a tie, it was an unusual look but one he was able to pull off. "What's so urgent?"

"You told him about Paul Gonsalves?" I asked Carlos.

"I told him."

Cody stood there, defiant.

"We need to talk," I said.

"Why are you talking to my friends?" His tone was not friendly.

"I'm an investigator. I talk to people," I explained simply. "And you gave me a bogus phone number. Why don't you buy us lunch?" I suggested. "We should sit down somewhere and clear this up."

"I'm busy, and I don't have to talk to you," he said.

"No you're not, and yes you do," I replied. "I hate to be a bitch, but you're the president of a large casino. If you didn't need to talk to me, you wouldn't be standing out here on the hot pavement right now. Let's get past all this and you can try to talk me out of getting the cops involved. Maybe you can even convince me you're not a murderer," I added.

"You know I'm not," he snipped.

"I'm less certain now than ever," I said. I motioned with my hand at the expanse of the Strip in front of us. "Lunch. You pick the place."

Several seconds passed as Cody grudgingly weighed his options. Finally, he turned slightly, grimaced, and began walking south. "Okay," he said. "Capital Grille."

We walked in silence the two blocks to the Capital Grille, the upscale steakhouse chain, which was on the opposite side of the mall where we'd just had coffee with Paul Gonsalves. I was underdressed in my tank top and shorts, but they were used to that. It was Vegas. They might have made a fuss at dinner, but lunch on a Tuesday was different. The restaurant was only half-full, and I asked for a table in a deserted corner mostly hidden by the bar. It was the kind of lunch you didn't want being overheard.

The maitre d' showed us our table. I was used to drawing attention from people (a healthy mixture of appreciative leers and disapproving scowls), but Cody was clearly the star of our little traveling troupe. As we walked to our seats a number of people in the lunchtime crowd—women and men alike—stole furtive and not-so-furtive glances at him. It was like I wasn't even there. Either Cody was used to it or he didn't notice. I guessed he was used to it. We sat down in silence and ordered Diet Cokes when the waiter arrived. None of us were in the mood for small talk. The drinks came quickly, and we ordered lunch right away. Carlos and I ordered cheeseburgers and Cody got a lobster salad. I decided to begin the same way I had with Gonsalves.

"I have no interest in having you go to prison," I started. Cody's expression was stoic. I couldn't help imagining what would happen to a pretty boy like him behind bars. "And I don't care about how you arranged for your not guilty verdict, except for the fact that it is a useful thing to know."

He perked up at my innuendo. "What's that supposed to mean?" he asked.

"It means, now that I know about it, you've got to tell me the truth about everything else. And it means that you have to help me find out what I need to know."

"Or else?"

"Exactly. 'Or else' is the name of the game I want to play now." I leaned in and lowered my voice, hoping I could sell him on a lie. "So here's the 'or else.' I've already sent a sworn affidavit to my lawyer describing you and your friend on the jury. And there are . . . pictures. If you want that kind of thing making its way to the cops, I'm sure they'd be more than happy to try you again for murder. Hell, forget the murder. They could put you away for twenty years just for jury tampering."

"What kind of pictures?" he asked.

"They involve a recent pool party in a deserted subdivision on the east side. Use your imagination."

"Fuck you," he said a little too loudly. A fat woman in a bright printed top looked over at us and frowned disapprovingly. Cody's face was reddening. He gestured at Carlos. "Does this guy ever talk?"

"He's the strong, silent type," I said. Carlos narrowed his eyes and looked away. "Look, you don't have to like me. You do have to help me, though, and I need some answers."

"Or else," he repeated sarcastically, rolling his eyes for effect.

"Now you're catching on," I said. "For starters, I'll need to know who you were with on the night of the murder."

"Why?"

"Because I still think there's a reasonable chance you're guilty."

He sighed. He asked me for a pen and wrote down a name in all caps on the napkin: Oliver Radbourne.

"Is Oliver a real person?" I asked.

Cody was not amused. "You might have to take my word for it. Oliver has no clue about the whole thing. He was in town from London for a few days and I doubt he even heard about the murder or the trial afterwards."

"So it's basically a piece of worthless information," I said. "I track down this guy six thousand miles away and ask where he was five years ago on such and such a night, he'll have no idea."

"Probably. But if you mention my name, he'd be able to work out the dates and times, though. I haven't seen him since then."

"Sounds like you boys really hit it off," Carlos muttered.

Cody shot him a death stare while I stifled a laugh. I took the napkin and filed it away in the back pocket of my shorts. I'd probably throw it out later.

"You don't seem overly eager to help me prove your innocence," I said, stating the obvious.

"It's not that simple," he added.

"Why not?"

He looked me directly in the eye and lowered his voice. "Are you some kind of idiot? Do you think I like walking around having everyone think I'm a killer? Don't you think I would have cleared my name already if it was that easy? I don't need you, or anyone, swooping in here to help me."

I liked the stoned Cody much more than this guy. It was clear he wasn't finished with his little hissy fit, so I kept my mouth shut.

"Of course I want to prove to everyone that I'm not a murderer," he continued.

A light bulb went off in my head, and I couldn't help interrupting. "But if you disclosed your true alibi—Oliver Twist, or whatever his name was—your lovely wife would have amazingly excellent grounds for divorcing you and leaving you without a dime."

His eyes narrowed, but he didn't say anything.

"Which is why," I continued, "when the opportunity presented itself, you decided to try your hand at buying off the jury rather than asserting your actual alibi, which is pretty flimsy to begin with. You got to have it both ways. A verdict in your favor while holding on to the rich wife and casino."

He started shaking his head. "It's not that simple," he repeated. He sipped nervously from his soda. "You're forgetting something. The fact is, it's very convenient to have people think I'm guilty." Our food arrived, and we sat in silence while the waiter and an assistant arranged our plates in front of us. The waiter sensed we were in the middle of something and flashed a thin, efficient smile before disappearing.

"Convenient?" I prodded.

"Well *somebody* killed George Hannity," he said, digging into his salad. I thought about that for a minute while chewing my burger, which was medium rare and very good. Cody had a point. Assuming he was innocent, the situation had worked out pretty well for whoever the real killer was. Because everyone assumed Cody was actually guilty, the cops and DA's office never bothered to continue searching for George Hannity's murderer. The heat was off.

"It's convenient," I repeated, "and if that situation were suddenly stirred up by a nosey investigator, someone would be bound to get really pissed off."

"Now you're getting it," he said. He didn't look quite as angry as before. I hoped that getting some of these things off his chest was making things better.

"And that's where my interest goes beyond the purely financial," I said. "As I've already told you, someone is trying to get rid of me. They broke into my apartment and almost killed me. And I've had to move in with my uncle in Henderson," I lied. No sense letting anyone know where I was actually sleeping these days. "I don't think they're going to stop unless I get to them first."

He nodded. Carlos had dug in to his fries with both hands.

"My point is, even if you don't want to stir up the pot, that's a luxury I can no longer afford."

"What am I supposed to do?" Cody leaned back from the table. "I wasn't there, and I don't know who killed George."

"Suppose I believe you," I said. "Who else would have done it? Who had the motive to get rid of George?"

Cody put down his fork and paused. He chose his words carefully. "I don't know. A lot of people. George had a different vision of the place than almost everyone else." I wondered if it was possible to be any more vague. "Plus," he added, "it could have been a random act of street crime." It didn't sound like even he believed that theory. It was crap. I decided to answer his crap with a whopper of my own.

"I know about the money," I said suddenly. Both Carlos and Cody looked directly at me, and I thought I detected the beginnings of a wry smile working their way across Carlos' face. "The money" could have meant a million things, and I just wanted to see what Cody's reaction to the accusation would be.

"What money?" he asked. I didn't give him any points for originality.

"I think you know very well, Cody. You really expect us to believe that the casino is reporting all the money it should be reporting? I've heard otherwise. And now I discover you've been paying piles of money to Paul Gonsalves for years." I decided to let Cody make the obvious connection himself.

"I have money of my own," he said defensively. "I get three-hundred-thousand a year as president of the casino. My wife gets ten times that that just in dividends every year. I don't need to steal anything. Paul is small potatoes." I'd never heard anyone under forty use the phrase "small potatoes." It all sounded a little artificial.

"And I suppose your wife Amy is fine with you paying this handsome young man so much money?"

He shot me a withering look. "Very funny." He looked at Carlos for support, as though Carlos would take his side. Carlos began sucking suggestively on a French fry.

"Look," Cody continued, "obviously you're in way over your head here. I appreciate the fact that you have at least considered the possibility that I might be innocent. Most people haven't gone that far. But I'm not interested in helping you on your little project." He stood up abruptly. "You can send me the bill for lunch," he said, and walked out.

Carlos was smiling, obviously amused. "That is messed up," he said.

"You think so?"

"I mean, the guy basically admits to felony bribery and then won't help out the only person in town who doesn't think he's a cold-blooded killer."

"It *is* messed up," I agreed. "I guess he didn't believe me about going to the cops."

"You going to?" Carlos asked.

"Nope. Not yet anyways. I need to figure out who's after me, because it's obviously not Cody." We got the check and headed back to the car. I drove him home and Carlos' pretty young girlfriend was peering through the door when we got back. She waved and flashed a phony baloney smile at me.

Before he got out, Carlos coughed a loud *ahem* and started rubbing his fingers and thumb together, as though moving some invisible money back and forth. I had planned ahead, luckily. I caught his drift, fished a wad of bills out of my purse, and handed him close to a thousand in cash.

"Thanks," he said simply, and went inside.

Chapter 22

Back in my hotel room I flipped on the TV and fired up my computer. I had some loose ends to clean up. First, I picked out three photos of Cody and Paul Gonsalves in the pool and shrunk them down to a more manageable size. I then attached them to an email and sent them to Jeff Katz, whose email address was on the business card Rachel had given me. The photos weren't conclusive evidence of anything, but they showed that Cody and Paul were obviously close friends—or more. I explained in the email that Paul had sat on Cody's jury and told Jeff what to do with the pictures in the event I washed up on the shores of the Colorado River. I was sure Jeff would find the whole thing amusing.

After that I pulled up my Westlaw account and ran a real estate search on Cody's party house. The deed was held by a limited liability company called CAM Holdings, LLC, and I found that company registered in Delaware, with Cody A. Masterson as its principal agent and sole owner. I figured the limited liability company was probably just an extra step to hide his property from Amy.

I then ran some internet searches on Oliver Radbourne, the name Cody had written down for me at lunch. Cody had already lied to a jury and given me a bogus phone number, so there was no reason to believe he was telling me the truth about this guy. A three-year old photo of an Oliver Radbourne turned up in the online archives of *Yachting* magazine. This Radbourne was from London and definitely fit the bill in terms of the kind of man I expected Cody Masterson would hang out with, except that he was older than I would have thought. Late thirties, with a receding hairline—definitely not in the same league physically as Cody himself or his pool friends, but then again he was probably much richer. His name popped up in other publications, one of which described him as an "eligible" bachelor on the French Riviera scene in Cannes. A company called Radbourne and Associates, Ltd, an architecture and design firm specializing in hotels, had a web page listing contact information for a number of individuals, including the founder, Oliver Radbourne. It listed a London address and a long distance number I had no idea how to dial on my phone.

I called my cell phone operator to ask for help dialing the international number, and the operator put me through directly. I felt like June Cleaver. Radbourne was not in—the office was closed, the receptionist said—but she could take a message. I left my name and number but didn't expect a speedy callback.

After that I opened up my bookkeeping program and began trying to reconstruct how I'd spent my time on the case over the last several days. I had gotten sloppy about keeping records in the past, which always meant it was harder to collect on an invoice at the end of a job. Maybe Carlos had the right idea, I thought: only take cash, payable right away or at most within a few days. After about an hour of reconstructing the past week, I finished my calculations and hoped Rachel wouldn't mind paying me the $13,900 in fees and expenses I had racked up so far. Assuming she could eventually afford it, that is. All in all, I think I had earned it. The Flamingo suite and my intimate relationship with its mini-bar were another matter altogether.

Jeff called me while I was in the shower and ended his message with the instruction that I should call him back if I was still alive. Funny guy. Jeff wanted to see how I was doing and offered to take me out for dinner. I was still a little wary of his motives, but he'd been behaving himself very well lately. I told him I was dancing later and he could come in for a freebie. I didn't want to go to dinner with him, but I looked forward to running things past him and getting his legal take on things.

I got lost in the casino for a few hours to let the maids clean my suite. Talk about an expensive afternoon. The video poker gods were not with me, and the craps table wasn't much better. This is why I don't gamble very often. If I weren't staying on Jeff's VIP account, I think the hotel would comp me my suite for a week based on my losses that day alone. When I got back to my room I ordered takeout curry from my favorite Indian place. The skinny Indian delivery boy recognized me and gave me a funny look, probably confused about why I was staying in a hotel when I lived in a condo across the street. But, as usual, he didn't say a word to me.

I floundered around for awhile after dinner and got to Cougar's early. I didn't really feel like dancing, but I knew it would take my mind off things. It proved to be even slower than usual for a Tuesday night in July, and I spent more time on stage than I had in months. The wad of singles I earned dancing on stage wouldn't put a dent in what I'd lost at the tables that afternoon. I even put on my tallest pair of hooker heels, but they didn't seem to help.

Things picked up around nine-thirty when some elderly Japanese men arrived. From experience, I knew they tended to prefer blondes—their image of the perfect American woman was Pamela Anderson, circa

1996. But Mr. Takada took a shine to me and had me on his lap for a good half-hour. I think I outweighed him by twenty pounds. I probably cut off the circulation to his legs, but he didn't seem to mind.

The Japanese left by 10:30 and I pondered leaving early. That was the nice thing about being an independent contractor: I could lay myself off anytime I felt like it. But soon enough an attractive sandy haired guy in his late twenties approached me while I was walking back from the locker room for one last go-round on stage.

"How much for a lap dance?"

"For you?" I gave him a once-over and smiled. "Half price. Twenty bucks."

"Actually it's for a friend of mine. It's his birthday. Here's a hundred." He flashed a tight smile and pressed a hundred into my palm. "He's with another girl back there already. They're just finishing up." He seemed a little nervous, but that was nothing unusual. A lot of guys weren't comfortable talking to women at all, much less nearly naked women in four-inch stilettos.

I was disappointed that the cute guy didn't want a dance, but work was work. I put the money in my hidden pocket and headed over to the back room. Mandy was the only girl dancing back there. She was a real professional, a stunning blonde who would have been a Victoria's Secret model except for the fact that she was only five-foot-four. She was perched on the lap of a guy in dark gray slacks and nice looking dress shoes. He was facing away from me and seemed to be enjoying having Mandy's 34-C's in his face. I caught her eye. She nodded and flashed me a one-minute sign with her hand.

Mandy climbed off the man exactly a minute later. He tipped her and she patted his head affectionately when she left. Easy money. She must have told him I was on my way because he didn't move. He sat rigid in the chair like a boy about to get a hair cut.

I walked over and stood next to him. "Tonight must be your lucky night," I said, resting my hand on his shoulder. I moved in front of him to face him and began to pull off my flimsy top. It was then that I looked down at his face for the first time. He was about forty-five, with bushy brown hair and a mustache straight out of the seventies. There was a long gash on the left side of his face, and his left eye was swollen. I inhaled sharply and froze. He was staring back at me with murderous eyes, and I froze and couldn't shake his glassy eyed glare. It was the Brawny man. I screamed.

I was still screaming when I turned to flee. I got nowhere. He grabbed onto my forearm and held me with a vise grip. There was no wriggling out of that grasp this time, and I didn't have a Corona bottle to use as a weapon. Even in my panic, I wondered what he was thinking. Security would jump on him within ten seconds. And then I saw the knife in his left hand. It wasn't just any knife, either: it was an 8" hunting knife with an elongated point. I didn't see his arm move until it was almost too late. At the last instant I managed to duck enough that the blade missed my throat and cut into my shoulder. I shrieked as it sliced through muscle and soft tissue. Tears welled up in my eyes, but I wasn't going to give him a second swing at me. I stomped down and, somehow, landed true on his right foot. My stiletto heel must have punched right through his leather shoe because he let out a loud snarl and let go of my arm. I ran.

Two security guys raced in past me as I fled of the back room. I watched the scene unfold. My attacker was obviously in pain, but he wasn't down. He was limping quickly towards the fire exit, but the security guys managed to drag him to the ground before he got out. DeShawn, a six-four former BYU lineman, belted him clean in the face, and Brawny man's head hit hard against the floor. I wasn't in the mood to watch the rest of it.

I ran downstairs to the locker room and grabbed my things. I found some paper towels and cleaned up my shoulder. It hurt like a bitch but it looked better than I would have thought. It stopped bleeding with a little pressure, so I crumpled up some paper towels and taped them over my wound with some giant band-aids.

There was no way I was going to finish my shift. They had found me at home, and now at work. I began wondering if I was even safe at the Flamingo. The fire alarm had gone off for a few seconds when the Brawny man tried to open the fire exit, and in their drunken state a lot of the customers seemed panicked. I found

Carlos at the front doors trying to calm people down. Once the dancers got back on stage, things slowly got back to normal and the customers went back to their seats.

I tapped Carlos on the shoulder. "Want to take me home?"

He raised his eyebrows. "I've been waiting years for you to ask me that."

I shot him a look. "Seriously. I need to get out of here. That guy tried to kill me. Again."

He put on his serious face. "Okay. It's not too busy."

"Don't bother punching out. Let's just go," I said.

He nodded. He said something to the other bouncer and took my arm to lead me out. It was a little heavy-handed, but it was comforting all the same.

"Let's take your car," I said.

We climbed into his black Mustang and he gunned it up the Strip. Halfway home, my cell phone rang.

"Raven?" The man's voice was frantic.

"Yes. Who's this?"

"Cody Masterson," he said, out of breath. "I'm in an ambulance on my way to the hospital."

"What happened?" I was wondering why he was calling me, of all people.

"Car accident," he said, before correcting himself. "Well, that's the thing. The truck came right at me. I was driving home right near my house, on Rampart Boulevard, and there's no median strip or anything." He was breathing heavily, and his mouth couldn't get the words out fast enough. "And the guy comes across the lane in this truck—it was like a dump truck or something—and swerves right into me."

"Are you okay?" I asked. I was having a hard time forcing my mind to focus on something other than my own pressing problems.

"My car flipped over when I swerved. I think I hit a fire hydrant, but the airbag kicked in. My arm feels broken, though. It got caught and turned around by the seatbelt when I flipped."

"Okay. And you think this was on purpose."

"I don't know how else to take it. The guy rammed right into me and then sped off. Someone must have seen me talking to you. Anyway, if I'm right, they won't stop until they finish me off. You have any friends with guns?"

I laughed grimly. "What about the cops?"

He paused. "I think we need to talk. You were right—I haven't been completely honest with you. I'm not exactly free to talk right now, though."

I imagined there was at least one paramedic in the a back of the ambulance with him. "What hospital are you going to?"

"Spring Valley," he said.

"Okay. Tell them to admit you under a John Doe name," I said, and hung up. I wasn't sure they could do that, but it sounded like a good idea. No sense making it easy to find him if someone was really trying to kill him. "We'll be there in fifteen minutes."

Carlos overheard the "we" part and shot me a pained look.

"That was Cody Masterson."

"Holy . . ."

"Exactly. He was in a car accident that he thinks was no accident."

"And?" he asked.

"How'd you like to drive me to Spring Valley Hospital?"

He could tell it wasn't really a question. He got into the right lane and turned up Tropicana. We drove in silence for a few minutes and then I explained what Cody had told me.

"You have a gun on you?" I asked.

He sighed for effect.

"Just for deterrence purposes," I said. "No one's getting shot."

"I don't have my big gun, but I've got my Glock in the trunk. Only a couple rounds in it, though."

"Good enough."

Chapter 23

We pulled into the hospital lot and Carlos dropped me at the emergency entrance.

"Oops," I said to no one in particular. I realized I had told Cody to use a pseudonym, but I had no idea what name he'd use. The lobby was surprisingly bustling for a Tuesday night, but then again I had no idea how busy a hospital was supposed to be. I hadn't been inside one since I was a kid.

I hit the callback button on my cell phone to dial the number Cody had just called me from. Cody didn't answer. He'd probably only arrived a few minutes before us, so he couldn't have gotten very far. And with a broken arm, it wasn't like they were going to take him to the geriatrics department or the psych ward. I decided to poke around the ER.

It didn't take long to find him. A clump of six or seven female nurses and other staff were crowded outside one of the exam room doors next to the ER. They were trading peeks through the door's small glass window. It wasn't hard to imagine who they were gawking at. I waited a minute for Carlos to come in after he parked. When he joined me, I nodded my head in the direction of the nurses pressing their noses up to the window.

"Gee, I wonder where Cody could be. Wait 'til those nurses find out he doesn't like girls."

"So much for patient privacy. Let's get him out of there before they eat him alive," I said.

We picked our way through the small crowd and I got a peek for myself. Sure enough, Cody was seated on the exam table, shirtless, his left arm already in a rudimentary sling. The examining doctor was a short, thin man with thick outdated glasses. He had Cody stretching his right arm back and forth, presumably to test for injury. I flashed my private detective's I.D. at the woman next to me, who seemed to be some kind of tech rather than a nurse. I nudged her out of the way and pushed the door open.

She stared at me but didn't say a word, and Carlos and I walked into the exam room. Cody looked up and appeared relieved when he saw me. He had a long gash below the jaw on his right side, but it didn't look too deep. Other than that and his broken arm, he seemed to have survived the crash unscathed.

"Excuse me, this is not a public area," the doctor said. His voice sounded detached, as though he knew his objection would be pointless. Cody spoke up.

"It's okay, they're with me." Cody said it as if he were in charge of hospital security.

I showed my I.D. to the doctor. "Is there another room we could take him? His security is at stake." I used my gravest voice. It was hard to appear grave when I had that much cleavage showing.

The doctor seemed bored by the whole thing and shrugged. "I'll get someone," he muttered, and left. I figured there wasn't too much that a Vegas ER doctor hadn't seen before.

Cody looked at Carlos inquisitively.

"He's got a gun," I said quietly. Cody nodded and directed his attention back to me. "So what are we going to do?" he asked.

"What we are going to do is get you out of here, and then we're going to talk," I said. "You need a cast?"

"Yeah. But they said it shouldn't take long."

I thought for a minute. "Carlos, how'd you like to play security guard?"

He shrugged.

"How about if you sit in the lobby and see if any bad guys come in. I'll wait with Cody. Call my cell if anything looks off."

He nodded and headed back to the lobby. When he opened the door, I noticed a few nurses and other women were still lingering outside the exam room.

"You have a fan club," I said to Cody. "It must be rough. Here you are, all scratched up with your arm in a sling, and you still can't keep them away."

Cody laughed for the first time. "It's good for the ego, I guess. A lot of times people think I'm in the movies or on TV, and they hang around trying to figure out who the hell I am. Sometimes I sign fake autographs."

"Do you sign them 'Lars Bergstrom'?" I asked.

He shot me a surprised look. Apparently his real name was a pretty well-kept secret.

I shrugged. "Why don't you start talking while we wait for someone to move you to another room," I suggested.

"Okay," he said. His eyes seemed a little wild, but he didn't seem stoned or anything. His voice was calm. "Basically, you were right about the money. I've been paying Paul Gonsalves since the trial. I didn't know him beforehand, but by chance we met up at a nightclub and I figured it was worth a shot. Now we're friends."

Cody's shorthand version was basically consistent with what Paul had told me, except I doubted that he met Paul "by chance."

"So you bribed a juror . . ." I prodded.

"Even though I was innocent. Yes. You have to remember that it didn't look good at the time. Everyone thought for sure I was going to prison. Even my lawyers. And I would have been eligible for the death penalty, too. Facing that, I think a lot of people would have done exactly what I did."

I tried to process what Cody was saying. It confirmed some of the assumptions I'd been working out in my head, and he seemed to be telling the truth. Finally.

The bored-looking doctor returned with a security guard and a bulky male attendant pushing a wheelchair. Cody obviously didn't need to be wheeled around, but they didn't seem to concern themselves with that detail. Cody proved to be a good sport. He put on the hospital gown they gave him and set himself down gingerly in the wheelchair.

"Room 604," the doctor said simply. He looked me over with a faint air of disapproval. "They can put the cast on him there," he said.

I grabbed Cody's shirt off of the exam table and followed them to the elevator and down a long, bleak corridor that seemed to have a few too many fluorescent lights overhead. The gaggle of gawking nurses had finally dispersed.

I was surprised to find a nurse already waiting for us in Room 604, and I left Cody and his shirt inside and stood guard outside the door. The security guard had sentried himself on a brown faux-leather chair in a mini-lobby near the elevator. He seemed fixated on a summer rerun of The Tonight Show. A young doctor soon arrived and joined the nurse in Cody's room. The whole procedure took less than a half-hour. It was either great service or they just wanted to get rid of us.

I thought about asking the doctor to check my own shoulder, but it had stopped bleeding and I wanted to get moving. Maybe I could bum some pain meds from Cody later, I thought.

Cody emerged a few minutes after the doctor left. He was a sight, and I tried to muffle a giggle. The sleeve of his yellow polo shirt had been cut open to allow room for the cast. The cast, which was bright blue, forced his arm to jut out upwards at a kind of half-salute. He had a line of stitches running from his neck to his jaw line, making him look like the gay Frankenstein. On our way out, we both gave a half-salute to the security guard and went down the elevator to the lobby. Carlos was lost in a dog-eared copy of *Golf Digest*.

"You're not even paying attention!" I scolded him. "Armed thugs could be after us and you'd never even have noticed."

"My divots aren't big enough," he said excitedly, like Archimedes shouting *Eureka*! in his bath tub. I didn't press for an explanation, but that didn't stop him from elaborating. "If you hit an iron shot right," here, he stood up and demonstrated his swing for us, "you should leave a long divot in front of the ball."

"You've got to hit *down* on the ball," Cody chimed in.

I rolled my eyes and grabbed both of them by the arms. Two of us had been victims of murder attempts within the last hour, and here they were talking about the dumbest game ever invented. I shook my head disapprovingly at Carlos. "Let's get out of here."

I watched out for any sign of trouble—*someone* had to—but the parking lot seemed clear. Apparently whoever was trying to bump off Cody either hadn't realized he was still alive or hadn't yet thought to check for Cody at the hospital. I didn't want to hang around too long in case the idea dawned on him.

Cody's injury meant he got to ride shotgun. I was relegated to the Mustang's embarrassing excuse for a back seat. I assumed Carlos didn't have the Jaws of Life in his trunk, so I decided not to try squeezing my legs into the three inches of clearance behind the front seat.

"Let's make this as quick as possible," I suggested.

Carlos nodded and hit the gas a little harder. "Where are we going, by the way?" he asked.

"Cody still has some things he needs to say," I prodded. "Let's get us back to the Flamingo. We can disappear in that place and no one will give us a second look."

Carlos checked his watch, which prompted me to do the same. It was just after 11:45. "You got a hot date, Carlos?" I asked. "It's not like you have to be at the office early tomorrow." I realized it would be better to have company tonight—armed company—than be alone with a guy who was either the target of a recent murder attempt or a murderer himself.

"No, I'll join you," he said. He didn't sound too enthusiastic. We let the valet park the car, but before extracting myself from the back seat I grabbed a crumpled baseball cap I'd seen peeking out from under the seat. I thrust the cap at Cody. I couldn't cover up the royal blue cast jutting out from his yellow shirt, but I thought the baseball cap might at least disguise Cody's face and hide his golden hair. Cody frowned, but he got the drift and put the hat on so the brim covered half of his face. Carlos discreetly found his gun in the trunk and shoved it underneath a jacket to hide it.

We headed to the elevators and up to my suite without incident. Carlos whistled dramatically when we entered my suite. "So *this* is how you roll," he said, impressed. "Just like I imagined it." He went over to the bedroom and made a show of feeling the bed. Carlos looked at me suggestively. I flipped him off.

Cody made himself as comfortable as was possible in one of the leather chairs facing the bed. He wriggled a little bit, as though steeling himself for the Spanish Inquisition.

Carlos stared out the window at the Strip below, and I plunked myself down on the bed to face Cody. "Why don't you finish the story you were telling me at the hospital."

Chapter 24

Cody paused for a few seconds. "I need to take a pill," he said simply. He fished around in his pocket and produced a small foil pack with three pills in it. He went to the bathroom and got himself a glass of water, and when he returned to the same seat he exhaled and looked directly at me. I went into the bathroom and examined the foil pill pack. Tylenol with codeine.

"Anything I tell you," he said, "you can't tell the cops. Okay?"

I nodded. I wasn't exactly in a position to promise him anything, but I decided to fake it. "I'm only interested in figuring out who killed George Hannity and who's been after the two of us. I don't do very well in this business if I go running off to the cops all the time." I hoped that would satisfy him.

He leaned forward and seemed relieved to have the green light to talk. "Basically, you've really stepped in it big time," he said. Carlos grabbed a six-dollar can of soda out of the mini-bar and sat down to pay attention.

Cody continued. "It started, as far as I know, about five or six years ago. I wasn't there yet, so this is just what I heard. Phil d'Angelo, the manager, was in the process of taking over the financial end of the casino from a guy named Melvin Block, who was this old Jewish guy with a terrible comb-over. Really old school, and probably mobbed up. But I only worked with him for a few months before he retired. I think he's living out of state now."

I nodded encouragingly, but saw no reason to let him know I'd talked to Block only last week.

"So they were in the process of upgrading all the slot machines, which they're doing all the time. People want more glitz, different themes, all that kind of stuff. One year Elvis machines are hot, and the next year they want Wheel of Fortune slots with Vanna White on them. The latest craze is vampires. Anyway, the management is always reconfiguring the layout of the floor, forming the machines into rows, circles, straight lines, that sort of thing. It's like some weird voodoo science, always trying to guess what arrangement will make people gamble more."

"A million ways to separate chumps from their money," Carlos chimed in.

Cody ignored him. "Anyway, one day a new shipment arrives for slots that are supposed to be squeezed into a corner where there hadn't been any slots before. Twelve of them. And Phil gets the bright idea: why do we have to tell the owners about these slots? George Hannity had been out of town for a month on some cruise with his wife, so he wasn't paying close attention. Neither was Amy. Mel Block might have figured it out, but he was close to getting pushed out, so Phil figured he had free reign. There are seven-hundred-some machines on the floor, and they're always changing things around, so no one will notice if a few of them aren't on the grid, right? That was the plan. Instead of skimming off the total take, Phil basically started his own little twelve-machine casino inside the Outpost."

Carlos was nodding appreciatively. "Nice," he said.

"They aren't in a prime location," Cody said, "but the machines bring in a daily profit of around three hundred bucks. Each."

I tried to do the math in my head, but Carlos beat me to it. "That's thirty-six-hundred a day times three-sixty-five. That's close to a million-five a year," he said.

Cody nodded. "Tax free."

"How did Phil get the money out?" I asked.

"That was the main problem. The machines can hold thousands—much more than in the old days, because most people use paper money rather than coins. And there are different security shifts responsible for emptying different banks of machines, so no one ever thought it was unusual that our special bank of slots wasn't being emptied."

"But someone had to empty them eventually," I said.

"Right. Phil needed a partner, so he brought in a guy named Eddie Holman, who's now the head of security."

"We've met," I said cryptically.

Cody continued his explanation. "Holman had worked his way up from the cage and knew exactly how and when to empty the machines quickly, and each time he brought with him a new employee to help, usually some trainee who wouldn't have a clue what was going on. And I bet if you checked, a lot of the security tapes from those nights have mysteriously gone missing."

It was beginning to make some sense, I thought. "And now you're getting to the good part, right?" I asked.

"What do you mean?" Cody asked.

"I mean, the part about how you've been tapping into this bottomless gold mine yourself. You said they were stealing from the owners, but you're one of the owners now. Or at least your wife is."

He was silent for a few seconds. "I guess that's true. I found out about it almost by accident pretty soon after I started working there. I'm not as dumb as people think, and when I went over the floor map one day I noticed things didn't add up."

I chuckled. "Oops," I said.

"Yeah. So we've been splitting the pie a few ways. Phil gets the largest slice, and Holman and I take twenty grand a month."

"Okay," I said, "so that's how you fund your monthly contributions to Paul Gonsalves, and it explains how you pay for a second house. All without your wife knowing. What does it have to do with George Hannity's murder?"

Cody nodded, seeming to anticipate the question. "I don't have a clue," he said. "I don't know if George found out about it or what, but nobody told me anything about any murders. All I know is one day I woke up and there was a crime unit digging in my backyard. Five months later I was in court looking at a death sentence."

I had been thinking about it while Cody was talking. "Well, it stands to reason that whoever tried to kill you tonight is on the same page with the guy who's been trying to kill me. It seems like nobody wants the boat rocked. By the way, what's this guy's name, anyway?"

"Who?"

"Works for Eddie Holman. He's got brown hair, huge mustache. Looks like Jeff Foxworthy on steroids."

Cody laughed. "That's Dave Kootz. He basically does everything Holman says. And I mean *everything*."

I decided to leave that one alone. "So your theory is that Holman or d'Angelo are after you because they think you're going to give up what you know about your little money skimming operation?"

"Yeah, I do. But it's not just that. If Holman or d'Angelo were behind Hannity's murder, they'd be scared to death that I was talking to you. Like I said earlier, it's really convenient for the true killer that everyone assumes *I* did it. If they think I'm going to start claiming to be innocent again, it upsets the applecart."

I nodded. "So they'd want to kill both of us. Quickly. The problem is isolating who it is."

Cody was silently pondering things.

I continued thinking out loud. "Obviously this Kootz guy is doing the dirty work. He's not a problem anymore. I think DeShawn put him out of commission when he tried to run away. But I'm guessing he's not doing this on his own. The question is whether he's working just for Holman or if this goes all the way to d'Angelo."

Cody nodded. "We can't exactly go back to our normal lives without figuring that out," he said. "I mean, they're obviously following us. If we don't get to the bottom of it now, they're going to get us first."

He was right. I wanted to end this as soon as possible. "I could call the cops and file a complaint against this Kootz guy, but that would only be a short-term fix. We need to see how far this goes and bring everybody in at once."

Carlos nodded gravely.

A half-baked idea was forming in my mind. "Let me ask you, Cody: how'd you feel about acting as a double-agent?

He fixed me with a skeptical look.

"We're running out of options. You've told me everything, but we can't just sit around holed up in here forever."

He shifted uneasily in his chair.

I decided to flesh it out aloud. "Tonight was just a car accident, right?" I asked rhetorically. "*You* know it was intentional, but they don't know you know. You could brush it off and play it cool. Pretend you have no idea anyone was deliberately trying to hurt you."

"Okay . . ." he said, tilting his head slightly. He was still a little wary.

I pressed on. "What if you call one of them up and tell him you're meeting with me tonight. Tell them I've solved the case, and I'm going to disclose the identity of George Hannity's killer to you."

Cody frowned. "Then they'd just come after both of us," he said.

Carlos moved closer. "Exactly." He was smiling. "I think I get it," he said. "You can't go after them, because you don't whether it's d'Angelo or Holman. But you can get them to come to you. With this Kootz guy out of the way, one of them will have to show himself. He'll know you guys have been talking to each other, but he doesn't know you know that."

Cody pursed his lips and lifted an eyebrow in a show of puzzlement, but it seemed he was catching on, too. "Then what?" he asked. "That sounds pretty dangerous."

"We can take some precautions," I said, even as I was thinking through the options. "The thing is, you're not the only target anymore. I'm a target too. If the killer found out we were both going to be in the same place, he couldn't resist the opportunity to bump off both of us at the same time."

Cody wasn't following.

"Ever since Kootz tried to kill me on my balcony, I've been holed up here at the hotel. They haven't been able to find me here, at least not yet. They managed to find where I worked, but tonight was probably their last chance. They know I'm not going back there now."

Carlos stood up. "So they're desperate. Whoever it is would jump all over this if he found out where you guys were going to be and when you were going to be there." He seemed impressed with the plan.

"He could kill two birds with one stone," Cody said.

"And we're the birds," I said grimly. "One more question. If you had to guess between Holman and d'Angelo, who would you take?"

"For what? Hannity's murder?"

I nodded.

"Who knows? Both could have done it. Phil had more to lose if the skim was discovered—money, job, that sort of thing—but Holman is pretty much a thug. And obviously they *both* could have been in on it," he concluded.

"Call Holman," I said. It came out more decisive than I actually felt. "If he shows up alone, he's probably in this by himself. And if he doesn't show up at all, it means d'Angelo's probably our guy."

My mind was running through a list of possible places to stage a late-night rendezvous, but it was coming up blank. It couldn't be a public place, because I wanted some privacy and space to confront whoever showed up. What I needed was an office, but I didn't have one. Cody could tell Holman he was meeting me at my office, and then we could lie in wait for the killer there.

My mind wandered for a minute before I realized I knew someone with an office: Jeff. I hesitated to extract another late-night favor from him, but I didn't have much choice. Luckily, he was still awake when I called.

"You want to use our office for *what*?" He sounded reluctant.

I glossed over a few of the details. Especially the part about Carlos and his Glock.

"Okay," Jeff finally agreed. "But not the one downtown. We rent a suite of offices in a building about five miles east of the Strip. It'll be deserted at this hour. There's a big parking lot coming off a long driveway from the street. Nice and private. Let me just look up the security code."

"Is there a sign outside?" I asked.

"A sign?"

"Something listing who occupies the building," I explained.

He thought for a second. "I don't think so. It's just a nondescript brown office building."

It sounded as good a place as any. If there was no sign out front, they wouldn't realize I didn't actually have an office in the building until it was too late. Jeff gave me the address and the security code. I thanked him and wrote it down. I made a few more phone calls before we left. I woke up Lieutenant Sean Whelan, but he would forgive me if this all worked out. I turned to Cody.

"Ok, call Holman and tell him you're meeting me at my office at 3221 North Nellis Boulevard at 1:30 a.m. That gives us an hour. If he asks why we're meeting in the middle of the night, it's because I'm going to the cops first thing in the morning to have them arrest George Hannity's killer. And remember, you were in a car accident and you don't suspect foul play. As far as they know, you're on their side."

Cody looked like he still wasn't getting the whole plan. Maybe it was the codeine, or maybe my plan was just that crazy. I tried my best to explain it again.

"I figure that Holman is in this up to his eyeballs anyway, so even if he didn't murder George Hannity himself he's got to know that d'Angelo did it. He seems like a loyal lackey, so he'll tell d'Angelo about our little meeting tonight, at which point they'll probably both come over and try to kill us. But if Holman did do the murder by himself, he'll probably come alone. Either way, we have a good shot of finding out who killed George Hannity and ending this madness tonight."

Cody nodded, still looking a bit apprehensive. "Won't he suspect a trap if I call him out of the blue?"

"Not if you play it right. You're in on the skim too, remember? So you're just as anxious as he is to shut me down. And having them think I know the murderer's identity will light a fire under him."

Cody cracked a faint smile of satisfaction. "Actually," he said, "that might work."

Chapter 25

My first call had been to the Flamingo valet to order up my car, so when we got downstairs it was already waiting for us. With little traffic at that hour, the drive over to Nellis Boulevard took less than ten minutes. We drove into a deserted parking lot surrounding a dated and boxy three-story office building. I parked prominently out front and the three of us headed to the front door.

We were early, which would give us enough time to survey the office building before the guest of honor showed up. I punched in the key code Jeff had given me and walked in the main entrance. I fiddled with the door to make sure it stayed unlocked.

The inside of the office building was mostly brown painted brick. The three of us walked through the lobby, which was an open atrium with skylights on the ceiling above the third floor. The walls were broken up only by a few dated wall hangings and a large indoor palm. The front of the lobby was a wall of windows on both sides of two oversized glass doors. I thought it must be expensive to keep the space cool in summer. The only light came from a few safety lights attached to EXIT signs near the doors. We headed up a set of thick wooden slat stairs, which led to a corridor overlooking the lobby below.

"Okay, this will work fine," I said. "Cody, you can wait up here out of sight, and Carlos and I will be ready downstairs for whoever shows up." Cody was too injured to be useful, and the codeine had made him a little loopy. He didn't protest being left out of the fun.

"Let me see your cell phone," I said.

He handed it over. I found the voice recorder button.

"You know how to use the recording function? If I get him to start talking, press record and see if we can get a confession on tape."

Cody nodded solemnly and Carlos and I went back downstairs to look around. I found the switch for the chandelier and turned it on. On the wall opposite the entrance was a large black directory board listing the building's occupants. In addition to Jeff's law firm, the directory listed a pair of psychologists, an insurance agency, and a number of other lawyers. A commercial real estate agency seemed to occupy the entire basement floor.

"So they'll think you have an office here?" Carlos asked.

"Yeah."

"Then the first thing he'll do is walk over to the directory to see what floor you're on."

I nodded. "If we're lucky, he'll stand here for a few seconds scratching his ass while we sneak up on him."

"All I need is two seconds," Carlos said confidently.

We looked around the rest of the lobby. Off to the right of the building's entrance a hallway extended off of the lobby. Carlos seemed to pick up on my thought. He walked in that direction and eased himself into the hallway's shadows.

"Can you see me from there?" he asked.

"Yes, barely, but I *know* you're there and I'm looking for you. I think we'll be fine." From the edge of the hallway he had a clear line of sight towards the entrance and the building directory. There was a dim safety light at the far end of the hallway, but it didn't expose Carlos too much.

"Two questions," he said. "One, what if this guy pulls on me and I have to shoot him?"

"Hopefully you'll be able to sneak up on him and grab his gun before he has a chance," I said. "Assuming he even has a gun."

"Hmm," he muttered, unconvinced. "And what if it's more than one guy?"

"Let's hope it's not. If they both show up, though, you'll have to surprise them from across the lobby and convince them it would be fatal if either of them reached for a weapon."

Carlos fixed me with a reproachful look. "You don't pay me enough to do this," he said scoldingly. "And isn't it about time you got a damn gun of your own?" He was probably right on both counts.

It was twenty after one now, and Carlos and I faded back into the shadows to watch for Holman or d'Angelo to show up.

One-thirty came and went without any sign of either of them.

Carlos was twitching impatiently. "Where's your buddy?"

"Be patient."

"This is crazy, you know. I'm hoping they don't show and we won't have to put this half-assed plan to the test."

I was beginning to agree. Maybe we could all go out and have a few pints to wash away our pent-up nervous energy. It was possible, I admitted, that Holman had better things to do in the middle of the night than think about my whereabouts and a three-year-old murder. Cody had said Holman only grunted when he told him he was meeting with me.

"At least one of them has got to show up," I said.

After another ten minutes of waiting in suspended silence, Carlos had had enough. He had managed to inch imperceptibly closer and closer to me as the minutes had ticked by. He was now literally breathing down my neck.

"Don't touch me," I said. His hand had found its way to my waist.

"Just passing the time," he pleaded. He pressed himself gently against my ass.

"Is that your gun?"

"You tell me."

I sighed. "When I was a kid, we had a dog named Tex that my dad refused to have fixed. The dog was so horny that he would try to have sex with himself in the mirror. A lot of the kids in the neighborhood thought it was hilarious to let Tex hump their legs."

"This was before PlayStations existed?"

"Hell, we didn't even have Nintendo. The point, though, is: Tex was a good dog. We let him have his fun."

"And?"

"If you were a dog, we'd have put you to sleep by now. This isn't exactly the best time to make a move on me."

"Fuck," he whispered. It wasn't a reaction to being shot down but to the two strikingly bright beams of light now streaming into the lobby from the parking lot. The car's headlights illuminated the entire space with an eerie halogen glow, and the hum of its engine whirred audibly as it idled outside. We couldn't see the car from our position, but as the seconds ticked by it seemed like the driver was reluctant to get out. Was he waiting for someone? Was he scoping out the place?

The last thing I wanted was someone who suspected a trap.

After a few seconds the car's engine revved loudly and the headlights swung around to the left as the car backed up and turned around. Was he leaving or was he just positioning the car for an easy getaway? Carlos looked at me and shrugged. We waited another minute, listening for the tell-tale sound of a car door closing, but that sound never came.

From our vantage point we could see the inside of the lobby doors but not anything outside, and the panel of floor-to-ceiling windows next to the glass doors ensured we'd be spotted if we tried to peek. We stayed put.

"Sounds like he left," Carlos said.

"Hold on." I secretly hoped Carlos was right.

Carlos nudged me. The left-hand lobby door had swung outward silently, in slow motion. A man's leg stepped tentatively across the threshold. Carlos and I both instinctively crouched even lower in the shadows. The man closed the door without making a noise. For a split second I worried he would look to his right and see us, but he stood there looking straight ahead. He seemed to have zeroed-in on the building directory on the other side of the lobby, just as Carlos had predicted. As he moved into the center of the dimly lit lobby, I finally recognized the tall bulky figure with white hair.

Carlos looked at me.

Holman, I mouthed.

He nodded. I think we were both relieved that Holman was alone.

As we'd hoped, Holman had his back towards us as he studied the directory in search of my office, and Carlos wasted no time in creeping towards him silently. I followed behind, but kept my distance. Holman was wearing an untucked black polo shirt and jeans, but I was more interested in the gun he wore in an open holster under his right arm.

Holman was searching to find my name on the building directory. It took him ten or fifteen seconds to realize I wasn't on the directory, and he let out a curse of frustration under his breath. That was Carlos' green light. Before Holman knew what hit him, Carlos sprung on his back and laced his arms underneath Holman's, holding him in a kind of three-quarter nelson grip. Holman began swearing and flailing around wildly, trying to throw Carlos off.

I took my cue and tried to center a punch right at Holman's nose, but he spun away and I caught him full in his right ear. I hadn't punched anyone since sixth grade, but it was enough to stun him. He stopped spinning long enough for me to grab his gun away from him while Carlos had him immobilized. I punched him full in the face again for good measure.

"What the fuck?" he sputtered. He hadn't recognized me yet.

"Shut up," I said. I tucked the gun into my waistband, hoping I didn't look too ridiculous. Carlos jumped off Holman's back and shoved him against the wall. While Holman staggered to stand up, Carlos drew his Glock and pointed it at Holman's head, which was now spattered with his own blood.

His body heaved as he tried to catch his breath. "Fuck you," he hissed.

"Real original. I suppose you're here to kill me the same way you killed George Hannity."

"I never killed anybody," he spit.

"Right. So why show up here in the middle of the night with a loaded handgun?" I asked. Carlos cocked his Glock suggestively, and I hoped the sound of ready steel would get Holman in a more talkative mood.

"None of your business," he grunted. "Who's your gangster boyfriend here?" He sneered at Carlos. A Mona Lisa smile appeared on Carlos' face. He cocked his head to one side and suddenly pulled the trigger. The unexpected explosion of brick and lead was deafening, and shards of crushed brick flew in every direction. When the dust settled, a crater in the wall appeared about a foot from Holman's left ear. Holman looked at me beseechingly, as though I would protect him.

"My boyfriend here is an illegal with nothing to lose," I lied. "He can be very violent, unfortunately," I said with mock sadness. "Now why don't you tell us how you murdered George Hannity." That was the cue for Cody to begin recording with his cell phone.

A thin mist of brick dust cast a haze throughout the lobby, and the pungent smell of fresh gunpowder wafted through the air. Holman lifted his mangled face up again. "I told you, I never killed anybody. Just let me go and I swear I will leave you alone forever."

Carlos and I shared a brief chuckle at that suggestion, at which point Carlos pointed the gun directly at Holman's head. I had hoped that the combination of a physical assault and a loaded gun would get Holman to talk, but that didn't seem to be working. At this point I wasn't sure what the next step was. It was tempting, but I wasn't going to let Carlos shoot Holman's face off.

It turned out the next step wasn't up to me. As Carlos re-cocked his gun, the throaty rumble of a truck engine began roaring towards us from the front of the building. Before I could react, a high-pitched crash pierced the air and the lobby became a cyclone of flying broken glass. Instinctively, I covered my head and bolted out of the way of the massive white SUV that had plowed through the front doors and was now barreling right at us. In the confusion, Holman managed to knock the gun out of Carlos' hand. Carlos recovered quickly, and the two men began wrestling on the floor for the gun before Carlos kicked it into a corner, where it got lost in all the glass and rubble.

In my tumble I must have cracked a rib, and I stood up slowly and half-dazed from the corner of the lobby. I began reaching for the gun in my waistband when a figure emerged from in front of Holman's white Escalade.

"Don't even think about it," the voice shrieked at me. It was Amy Masterson, and she was pointing a gun directly at my head.

I was stunned, frozen. The Escalade was still running, its halogen headlights piercing icy bright beams through the dusty air. My first thought was that Amy looked like a crazed wreck—either drunk or on drugs, or both. Her nipples were showing through a thin white camisole, and her gray shorts were way too short. Her pajamas, probably. The gun she was pointing at me seemed wholly out of place.

Apparently the sight of Amy wildly brandishing a gun had created a temporary truce between Carlos and Holman, and Carlos shot me a quizzical look as he eased away from Holman.

Amy kept one eye on me and turned slightly to face Holman. "Can't you do *anything* right?" She shrieked. She was beyond pissed.

"Amy," I said softly, trying to keep her calm. My mind raced, trying to find some explanation for the incongruous scene I was now a part of. Amy continued to point the gun directly at me, but she didn't say anything. It was obvious she hadn't planned what to do next. I decided my only hope was to seize the initiative.

"You got greedy," I found myself saying. Things were finally falling into place. She remained silent, just gaping at me, her eyes wide and jaw set. She clung tightly to the gun with both hands, and licked her lips nervously. She kept the gun aimed directly at the bridge of my nose.

"You could have just bumped off your brother George and gotten the whole casino for yourself. Nothing novel about that—they did that kind of thing back in biblical times." I was struggling to keep my voice calm. I was stalling for time, and I hoped that my monologue might keep her distracted. "But you decided that wasn't enough. Once you learned your husband wasn't really interested in you, you wanted to get rid of him, too. The problem was that you were stuck with him—he'd clean you out if you divorced him." I hoped Cody wouldn't stand up and protest. If Amy suddenly saw him, there was no telling what she'd do with that gun.

Her eyes narrowed a bit, and she shifted her weight from leg to leg. It seemed she was comprehending what I was saying, but her body began trembling slightly and her arms began weakening under the gun's weight. No one moved. I kept talking.

"But you couldn't just get rid of Cody, could you? Another dead body would look a little suspicious, so another murder was out of the question. But once it was clear no one suspected you of George's murder, you decided to frame Cody for the murder you committed and have Cody sent off to prison for life. That way you could divorce him, reap the benefits of your crime, and Cody wouldn't get a dime."

"You can't prove any of that," she hissed. Her face still looked defiant.

"You did it perfectly," I continued, working it out on the fly. "I have to compliment you. By testifying for Cody—even though it was a weak alibi—you made him dependent on you. Until this moment I couldn't figure out why you would stay married to each other, but that was the key. You were bound together by that lie. He couldn't divorce you and get your money because you could always retract your alibi testimony."

She continued sneering at me. "You don't know what you're talking about," she said. Her voice was barely a whisper.

"No, actually it's very simple. As long as you remained married to Cody, you could prevent him from testifying against you in court. It's called the marital privilege." I pulled that one out of my ass. "If the cops ever got around to pointing the finger at you for the crime, the only way to keep Cody off the stand was to stay married to him."

"Shit," Carlos muttered under his breath. Tears began running down Amy's face.

"Stop!" she yelled at me. Her big mouth was twisted into a sickening snarl.

"You probably never dreamed the jury would let him off, did you?" I pressed. She looked pathetic, but she hadn't quite admitted anything yet. I wanted her to say more while Carlos and Cody were listening. I hoped Cody's cell phone was recording everything. "It was easy for you to testify when it looked like he was guilty, but by then you hated Cody so much that you forgot the effect his face could have on people." It didn't hurt that Cody bribed one of the jurors, but I kept that little tidbit to myself.

"You bitch!" she screamed finally. Wait, *I* was the bitch? She inhaled audibly. Her whole body was shaking, and I was worried I'd gone too far to set her off.

Her eyes had been locked in on me, but suddenly she seemed distracted by something above my head. I turned to see Cody looking down at us from the second floor. He looked like some kind of angel, outlined in a halo of the reflected glow of the Escalade's headlamps.

Amy turned the gun on Cody, and for an instant I felt a pang of relief. Amy's face showed a kind of baffled rage. "You're supposed to be dead," she said matter-of-factly. It was the first thing she'd said that could be incriminating. I guessed she'd told Holman to ram Cody's car earlier. Or she'd done it herself.

Cody seemed unsure of what to say, but he looked as angry as she was.

"You killed your own brother?" he asked finally. He slurred his words, probably an effect of the codeine. "You were going to let me rot in prison just so you could have the whole casino to yourself?"

She sneered. "Actually," she said with unsettling calmness, "I was hoping you'd get the death penalty." With that she fired off a round at Cody, and the blast threw him back against the wall. His scream echoed through the lobby long after the sharp report from the gun stopped ringing.

I shouldn't have been shocked by the gunshot, but I was. As Amy turned the gun back to me my mind searched for any means of escape. I saw Carlos inching closer along the wall, but she saw him too and waved him off. He froze. I began slowly walking backwards as she took aim at me, and the last thing I remembered before the shot rang out was a strange crunching sound coming from my left.

My ears rang from the gunshot, which seemed louder than the last. A moment passed before I knew I was still alive. I felt myself for blood, and I felt a mixture of relief and confusion sweep over me as I realized I was okay. Amy was on the floor, somehow, rocking back and forth. Blood poured sickeningly from the stump where her right arm used to be.

"Nobody move!" boomed a voice on my left. It was Lieutenant Sean Whelan. If I hadn't phoned him earlier, I might not have recognized him. The last time I'd seen him, he'd been plastered and probably at the tail-end of a three-day bender. Now he had an all-business expression, and he was wearing a bullet-proof vest.

Whelan nodded at me gruffly and pointed his weapon at Carlos.

"He's okay," I said. "The other guy is trouble," I said, pointing at Holman. "There's another guy upstairs. He's been shot. Can you call in an ambulance?"

"You do it," Whelan said. "Just dial 911."

I did. They said it would be five to ten minutes.

Whelan moved towards the crumpled figure of Amy Masterson and picked her handgun off the floor, the whole time keeping his gun pointed at Holman. Holman instinctively held his hands in the air, and he eased himself backwards to lean against the wall. I discreetly felt the front of my shorts to see if my bladder had emptied. Somehow, I was dry.

"What the hell is that thing?" I asked, nodding at Whelan's gun.

"Shotgun," he said, reporting the obvious. "Beretta M4, if you're keeping score. When I saw the Escalade had driven right through the front doors, I figured I better not come in here with a pop gun."

Whelan looked Amy over and nudged her onto her back with his right foot. It might have otherwise been a crass gesture, but Whelan had to keep one eye on Holman. Amy's right arm now ended just below her elbow, and there was no sign anywhere of the remains of her hand and wrist. She seemed to be going into shock, and I wondered if the ambulance would have room for both her and Cody. That would be a scene.

"She'll survive, but she'll have to become left-handed," Whelan said.

With the building's front doors and windows smashed in, we were now standing in an open-air lobby. A faint desert breeze wheezed in from outside, and it carried with it the sound of sirens approaching from a distance. I began breathing a little easier. Whelan walked around to survey the damage, his heavy black shoes crunching the broken glass underfoot. He stuck his finger in the hole in the wall that Carlos had made with his Glock and then turned around to size up the hood of the Escalade, which was sprayed with a mixture of buckshot and blood.

Whelan looked at me quizzically, the faintest hint of a smile detectable on his face. He checked his watch. "I thought you said to come at two o'clock. It seems you guys started the party a little early."

"Sorry," I said. "The things I was planning to do might not have worked if an official police presence was here. So I gave ourselves a half-hour head start."

"Good plan," he said sarcastically. "Seems like you pretty much had everything under control. What were you planning to do, anyway?"

"Well, I thought there was a good chance we'd have to beat the crap out of somebody to get a confession."

"I see."

I laughed nervously. "Beyond that, I didn't know what to expect. Thanks for coming, though. Next time, I'll let the pros handle something like this." That was an understatement.

It seemed like Whelan had things under control, so I ran up the stairs two at a time. Cody was lying on his back and moaning. It looked like Amy had clipped his other arm. There was a hole in the shoulder of his shirt, but I couldn't see any blood soaking through.

"Are you okay?" I asked.

More moaning. I knelt down and checked his torso. It was his shoulder, all right, but there wasn't much blood at all. It looked like he would be okay, but he'd be dependent on someone for a long time. I lifted up his head and rested it on my thigh. He didn't seem to mind. I ran my hand through his hair and touched his face. It wasn't exactly how I had planned it, but what the hell.

I was stroking Cody's head softly when he opened his eyes and smiled at me. It made me all warm inside.

Carlos appeared at the top of the steps, shaking his head in disgust. "You're pathetic."

"*What*?" I asked innocently.

Chapter 26

"Whoa, slow down," Mike said at dinner the next night.

"Okay. I was saying my mistake was in focusing the whole time on who killed George Hannity, when I should have been looking for who tried to frame Cody for killing George. Once I guessed Cody was innocent, the real question was who would try to make it look like Cody was guilty. The most logical person was always Amy."

"But they were all up to no good, so how were you supposed to know?" He was being kind, trying to reassure me that I hadn't completely made a mess of things. "That was the confusing part," he continued. "Three of them were ripping the casino off, so nobody wanted to cooperate with you because that would end the good thing they had going. The newspaper made you into a hero," he added.

My last phone call the previous night had been to Leslie Trondheim, the *Review-Journal* reporter I'd taken to dinner a few weeks earlier. Les was wide awake when I reached her at 2:10 a.m., just as the ambulances arrived to take Amy and Cody to the hospital. I gave her the gist of the story and told her to rush a photographer to the hospital. She had managed to get the presses stopped for a late edition, and front page color images of a bloodied Cody and Amy Masterson greeted a stunned city the next morning.

Mike and I were sitting at a corner table at Lucello's, and it was very late. I had polished off a martini and he was politely sipping at a glass of red wine. I think it was evaporating faster than he was drinking it.

"Right," I continued. "Amy was calling the shots the whole time. And apparently Holman thought he was going to swoop in and become a multi-millionaire by marrying Amy when the time came."

"Really?" he laughed.

"That's what Lieutenant Whelan told me. That's why he was doing all her dirty work. She had him wrapped around her little finger."

Mike seemed impressed. In retrospect, I probably should have called him for additional backup the night before, but for some pigheaded reason I'd wanted to do it without Mike's help.

It was getting to be the awkward part of the night. Dinner was over, and after the week's events I didn't feel like sleeping alone.

"Mike, I need a favor. After all that's happened, I don't feel safe going back to the hotel by myself." The bad guys were all locked up by now, but that was a minor detail.

"I'll be happy to come with," he said. That was easy, I thought. Now how was I going to get him to stay? I doubted there was any tequila in the mini bar.

My car was still at the Flamingo. We paid the check and Mike drove us the five blocks back to the hotel. He had gotten quieter as the minutes ticked by. I wasn't doing us any favors either. Ninety percent of my job was asking questions. I couldn't think of a single one to keep the conversation going.

As we arrived at the door to my room, I fished through my purse for my key card.

"Nice place," Mike murmured. I was worried Mike was going to bolt before I could come up with another pretext to keep him. There was nothing that needed fixing, no pickle jars to open, no storm door in need of mending. Not even any termites that needed exterminating. As he inspected the view, my eyes drifted to the glasses on the bar. This is the part where I would ask him if he wanted something to drink. Where I would get him drunk and see if he even remembers what we did in the pool in San Diego. Where he would tell me he hasn't stopped thinking about me.

But I just stood there.

Mike returned from the window and made a show of checking the locks on the door. "I think you'll be just fine."

"Good," I said. We stood facing each other. His back was to the door now. He stood across from me, unsure what to do with his hands. He shoved them into his pockets.

"Well... thanks for tonight," I said, and before I even knew what I was doing, I brushed past him and found myself opening the door. I stood in the threshold, cuing his exit. "I'm sure I'll see you soon."

His eyebrows went up a touch, but other than that, he was his usual self—a blank slate. "Yeah. Good night," he said, almost in a whisper. He moved past me into the hall.

"See ya," I whispered back, but Mike had already disappeared around the corner. Talk about awkward. I stood in the doorway until I heard the elevator chime and the doors close. He wasn't coming back.

I sat on my bed pouting for a few minutes. For some reason I had just given the boot to the man I'd been lusting after. There'd be other chances, I told myself, but that night I just didn't feel like playing the role of the desperate pursuer, the woman who relied on gimmicks and booze to get what she wanted. I got up and started filling the hot tub. I shed my clothes and donned one of the hotel's extra-comfy bathrobes. It was time for one final raid of the minibar.

I chuckled to myself when I found two mini bottles of Cuervo tequila in the fridge hiding behind a half-bottle of wine. *Damn,* I thought. I was already having second thoughts about getting rid of him.

As I was getting up to turn off the water, a hesitant knock came at the door. My heart raced as I scurried to the door to check the peephole. It wasn't Mike.

Oh my God. I wasn't expecting this.

I flung the door open. "*Cody.*"

He smiled. "Your phone must be off. I've been calling all day." He still had his arm in a cast, but he was all cleaned up. It was incredible how good this man looked, and this was a guy who'd been *shot* only a day earlier.

"Come in, come in," I stammered.

"I brought you this." He held out a shimmering diamond necklace. "To say thanks. Thanks for believing in me. Sort of."

I reached out and took it, moving each diamond through the tips of my fingers. He took it back and fastened it around my neck.

"Wow," he said.

I checked it in the mirror, opening my robe half-way to see how it lay on my skin. It was a *wow,* that was for sure. I still hadn't said anything.

"You like it?"

"I *love* it, are you crazy? You didn't have to do this, though."

"I know. I just felt bad about how everything happened."

"Did you buy this with, uh . . ."

He chuckled. "With money I stole from the casino?"

I nodded sheepishly. It was a stupid question.

"Maybe. But we were stealing from a murderer, so I don't feel too bad."

His logic was impeccable. With diamonds like this, I could pretty much rationalize anything.

I thought for a second after an idea popped into my mind. I told myself *no,* that's not going to work. But some other part of my brain had seized control of my mouth.

"Say, Cody, do you like tequila?"

"I *love* tequila. Why?"

"Sit down. I'll show you."

I fixed him some tequila on the rocks and found some acceptable music on the clock radio. I moved towards him and began one of my most popular lap dance routines.

Before long, my robe came off. He was on the edge of his chair, and I pulled his head to my chest, enveloping it, as we moved together with the music. When the song ended, Cody seemed like he was trying to say something, so I let him up for air.

"You know," he whispered, "I'm . . ." He let it hang there.

I played dumb. "You're what?"

"I'm *gay,*" he whispered, almost apologetically.

I pulled his head back to me and whispered in his ear. "Not tonight you're not."

14279313R00159

Made in the USA
Lexington, KY
22 March 2012